BROGAN AND THE
JUDGE KILLER

Brogan McNally is minding his own business when Hank Carter, an outlaw on the run for the murder of a judge, tries to steal his horse. Brogan manages to foil Carter, but he meets up with him and his gang again when they attempt to rob a bank. Brogan thwarts the robbery, but Carter escapes and heads for an isolated homestead, where he badly injures the young owner, and kidnaps his wife. Brogan sets off in hot pursuit, but Carter's capture never seems certain.

Books by L. D. Tetlow
in the Linford Western Library:

BROGAN: TO EARN A DOLLAR
THIRTEEN DAYS

L. D. TETLOW

BROGAN AND THE JUDGE KILLER

Complete and Unabridged

LINFORD
Leicester

First published in Great Britain in 1993 by
Robert Hale Limited
London

First Linford Edition
published 1996
by arrangement with
Robert Hale Limited
London

British Library CIP Data

Tetlow, L. D.
   Brogan and the judge killer.—Large print ed.—
Linford western library
I. Title II. Series
823.914 [F]

ISBN 0–7089–7822–3

Published by
F. A. Thorpe (Publishing) Ltd.
Anstey, Leicestershire

Set by Words & Graphics Ltd.
Anstey, Leicestershire
Printed and bound in Great Britain by
T. J. Press (Padstow) Ltd., Padstow, Cornwall

This book is printed on acid-free paper

1

HANK CARTER'S fingers nervously played around the handle of his ancient Adams and his tongue snaked apprehensively across his dry, cracked lips. Some thirty or so yards in front of him, down the rock strewn slope, was the object of his nervousness, seemingly unaware of the danger lurking above him.

Hank had been wandering the desert for three weeks. His horse had died under him on the first week and since then he had been trying to find his way out of the searing hell-hole on foot. He had recently come to the conclusion that he must be travelling round in circles, since various rocks and other landmarks seemed sickeningly familiar.

He had cut some meat from the carcase of his horse, but it had putrified in less than a day. Since then he had somehow managed to survive on little more than tepid water and a single jack-rabbit he had had the good fortune to kill. Suddenly, with the arrival of the first human being he had seen in that time, his troubles seemed to be at an end.

The traveller's horse was the main focus of his interest, even though it did appear to be an old, weatherbeaten nag. At least he would be able to point it in the right direction and let it do the walking. The traveller? That was his hard luck; at best, provided the traveller did not offer any resistance, he would be left to find his own way back to civilization. At worst, Hank was quite prepared to kill him, he had killed three men already and was, as a result, a wanted man. How much was on his head he neither knew nor cared. His one aim was to put as much distance as possible between him and the men who were pursuing him.

The slope offered little in the way of cover, except for a small clump of dense brush to his right. This appeared to be the only chance he had of reaching his quarry undetected. He looked down at the figure below, vaguely thinking it strange that he had remained perfectly still ever since being observed; but Hank let the thought pass, his need for a horse overriding any logic.

Very slowly and, he thought, very quietly, he made his way along the small ridge until the clump of brush was directly between him and the man below. The slope seemed a little easier at that point and Hank quickly dashed for the cover of the brush, making quite a noise on the way, but by then he was past the point of no-return, his Adams was cocked and ready for use in his hand. He thought that perhaps the traveller might think the noise had been made by a rabbit or loose rock, which did happen from time to time for no apparent reason.

The figure still did not appear to have moved as Hank peered carefully around the clump of brush. Once again his tongue snaked across his lips as he started to ease himself forward. Only three or four yards now and he was ready to shoot if there was resistance.

"I reckon that's about as far as you go!" Hank froze in horror as he heard the familiar click of a hammer being cocked and almost at the same time felt hard steel pressing into the back of his head. "Drop your gun!" came the order from behind.

The man below had still not moved and Hank finally realized that he had fallen for one of the oldest tricks in the book.

Obediently Hank dropped his gun and laughed nervously, desperately trying to make light of the situation he now found himself in. A sharp nudge from the gun in the back of his neck indicated that he was to walk down the slope.

"Didn't intend no harm!" Hank croaked. "Just that I've been out here for about three weeks an' I ain't eaten nothin' in all that time 'ceptin' one old rabbit."

"There's food all about," replied his captor, casually. "All you gotta do is catch it or dig it up."

They were now standing by the fire of the traveller's camp and very slowly, Hank turned to face the man he would have willingly killed a few moments earlier and could not help but wonder if he was about to suffer the same fate.

"So what you gonna do?" Hank asked, staring into the hard, steely blue eyes of the older man holding him at gun point.

"You've got no horse," said the older man, "that what you wanted, my horse?"

Hank smiled thinly. "That an' whatever food you got . . . "

"Food? All you gotta do is ask; there's plenty, more'n enough for two. My horse? No deal, she stays with me. Three weeks you reckon you've been wanderin', I guess that must've been the remains of your horse I found a few miles back." The traveller motioned Hank to sit down on a rock and started to laugh. "City feller?" Hank nodded. "Guessed you must be. Your horse dies on you three weeks ago . . . "

"Two weeks," Hank corrected. "I'd been in this hell-hole a week by then."

"Two weeks! OK, two weeks ago your horse dies under you and since then you've been tryin' to find your way out . . . "

"That's about the size of it," admitted Hank. "I'd just about come to the conclusion I must be goin' round in circles."

"Mighty small circles too, I'd say. The remains of your horse can't be more'n four miles away."

"OK, so I'm a city feller, what don't know one direction from another. Mister, I was ready to kill you, just for that horse of yours. Yeh, I'll admit that much. I don't know how you did it, but I'll tell you this for nothin', if it'd been a straight draw an' shoot-out

6

there'd've only been one winner, an' it wouldn't've been an old saddle tramp like you."

"Good with a gun are you?" the saddle tramp asked, smiling slightly, but still keeping his gun trained on Hank. "Don't tell me, you belonged to one of them . . . what they call 'em — shootin' clubs? — I hear they go in for in the cities back east."

"Atlantic City's shootin' champion three years runnin'," replied Hank, somewhat proudly. "Fastest draw for four years runnin'."

The saddle tramp laughed loudly. "Fastest draw four years runnin', shootin' champion three years runnin' an' yet here you are, sittin' on a rock starin' down the barrel of a gun held by some old saddle bum. What happened?"

"You just got lucky!" snarled Hank.

"Mister, it's one thing bein' champion of whatever back east, but out here what counts more'n anythin' else is the ability to survive. Sure, bein' fast

7

with a gun an' a good shot counts for somethin', sometimes, but if you wanna survive you've gotta learn to use this country. You just fell for somethin' most folk would've smelled a mile off. Your fancy shootin' ain't no good to you at all if'n you is a dead man. You made enough noise to raise the dead when you was supposed to be sneakin' up on me . . ."

"Only noise I made was when I ran for that brush!" Hank protested.

"I'd heard you more'n half an hour ago," sneered the saddle tramp, "but then I'm used to it, I've lived like this most my life. I always reckon I can hear a fly land on a piece of shit from a hundred yards away. That's what counts see; fancy shootin' may be all right sometimes, but if you telegraph the fact you is comin' it ain't no use at all." He lowered his gun and sat on another rock opposite. "Now, as I see it there is only one reason a city feller finds himself in the position you're in: you're on the run from the law! What

8

you do, rob some kid's money box?"

"I killed me three men!" Hank was becoming defiant and felt that his claim would in some way impress his captor. "Fair fight though, but the law didn't see it like that, so I had no option but to run, an' headin' west seemed about the best idea."

"Yeh, I recognize you now," replied the saddle tramp. I seen your picture back in some town called Pine Ridge. Carter, I think that was the name, can't remember your given name."

Hank laughed sarcastically. "Someone had to read the name for you did they? Yeh, Carter, Hank Carter. So they've got a poster out on me already. How much am I worth?"

"You ain't worth nothin' as far as I'm concerned," replied the saddle tramp, "an' I don't need nobody to do my readin' for me. The law says you is worth five hundred dollars dead an' seven hundred an' fifty alive . . . "

"Cheapstakes!" snarled Hank. "They were three prominent men I killed."

The saddle tramp shrugged. "Maybe they was back east, but I don't reckon nobody's ever heard of 'em out here. Five hundred an' seven fifty, that's the price they've put on you. You'd better keep your eyes open for bounty hunters, they won't think the price is too small. What you wanna kill them fellers for anyhow?"

Hank laughed lightly and shook his head. "Lookin' back on it it don't make sense . . . "

"Most times it don't," interrupted the saddle tramp.

"There didn't seem nothin' else I could do." Hank smiled. "They were goin' to kill me, I know, I overheard them."

"An' that makes it a fair fight?"

"No, guess not. I thought it was them or me, so I picked them off one at a time. It wouldn't have happened if it hadn't been for Elizabeth . . . "

"Now it makes sense! There had to be a woman in it somewhere!"

"Yeh, she was the daughter of one of

the men I killed an' sister to the other two. She'd got herself in the family way an' was blamin' me. Maybe it was me, I don't know for sure, but I sure wasn't ready to get married like she wanted . . . "

"I ain't never had that problem!" the saddle tramp smiled. "I've had me my share of women, but I ain't never allowed myself to get tangled too deeply. OK, you made your point but you just blew your chance of gettin' a horse. Seein' as how I know your name, I guess it's only right you should know mine. McNally, Brogan McNally. Don't go much on the name McNally, just plain Brogan'll do fine."

"Do you intend handing me over to the law? Seven hundred an' fifty dollars, or even five hundred must seem a real fortune to a man like you."

"I already said," replied Brogan, "as far as I'm concerned you ain't worth nothin'. I ain't no bounty hunter an right now I've got me enough money for anythin' I want. No, as far as I'm concerned you're free to go on your way."

"Even though I would've killed you?"

"Didn't though, did you? Pick up your gun, you might need it."

Hank looked strangely at Brogan and then shrugged before going to pick up his gun. For a brief moment he was tempted to turn on the saddle tramp and kill him, but there was something in the way Brogan was holding his gun that told him he was likely to come off the worst in any shoot out. He grinned and holstered his Adams.

"Trustin' sort of feller ain't you! I might still try an' kill you."

"You can try!" replied Brogan with a disarming simplicity which in itself spelled danger to Hank.

"That food sure smells good." Hank smiled and changed the subject. "Did I hear you say there was more'n enough for two?"

Brogan handed Hank a metal plate

and a spoon. "Help yourself, I've had my fill."

Hank greedily ladled out a large helping, which left very little in the pot, grinned at Brogan and ladled the remainder on to the plate.

"Shame to waste good food. Since you've had all you want, I hope you don't mind if I eat the rest. Like I say, all I've had is one lousy rabbit in more'n two weeks."

"Be my guest," invited Brogan. "Makes a change to have someone appreciate my cookin'."

Hank said nothing else and set to tackling the full plate. It was not until he had almost finished that he spoke.

"I don't think I've ever tasted anythin' better!" he enthused. "What the hell was it, tasted kinda like lamb or veal?"

"Rattlesnake!" replied Brogan, studying Hank's face.

"Rattlesnake!" Hank exploded, coughing and spluttering. "What the hell you tryin' to do, poison a feller?" He immediately turned the food left on the plate on to the fire.

"An' just where the hell would I find lamb or veal out here?" Brogan laughed. "Ain't nothin' wrong with rattlesnake or any other kinda snake. Must admit I prefer lizard tail myself, but out here you gotta take what you can find."

Hank wiped his mouth and suddenly laughed. "I guess it's easy to see I'm city born and bred. I suppose I'll just have to learn what's good to eat and what isn't."

"If you intend livin' off the land it sure is useful to know what's good an' what ain't," said Brogan. "Don't worry 'bout it too much though, even most folk out these parts don't know how to feed 'emselves off the desert."

"OK, I'm convinced, you know more'n I do 'bout these things. So what now? If you aren't goin' to hand me over to the law, what are you goin' to do?"

"Leave you to make your own way,"

14

replied Brogan. "I'll point you in the right direction an' then it's up to you."

"You're goin' to leave me out here?" exclaimed Hank. "I ain't got no horse, remember!"

"You should be clear of the desert in about three days," said Brogan. "Providin' you don't go round in circles." He stood up and pointed towards a large peak on the distant horizon. "All you gotta do is head for that an' you can't go wrong. I ain't sure just what's beyond there, but it ain't desert that's for sure. I reckon you should be able to find a town or somethin'."

"I'm a wanted man, remember!" said Hank. "If they had a poster for me in that town you said, they'll probably have one in any other town."

"That's your problem." Brogan shrugged dismissively. "Since I ain't wanted for nothin' by nobody I don't have to worry. All I have to worry about is bein' chased out of town by some over zealous sheriff."

"If you ain't done nothin', why should they chase you out of town?" asked Hank.

"'Cos of what I am," replied Brogan. "I hear you've got tramps back east . . ." Hank nodded. "Well that's all I am, 'ceptin' I ride a horse. Most town folk have a thing against the likes of me, even though there ain't that many of us what ever do them any harm, leastways I ain't never done nothin' to nobody. I ain't never stole nothin' off nobody an' I ain't never killed a man what don't deserve it."

"An' you smell worse than a skunk!" Hank laughed.

"You don't exactly smell of roses," Brogan pointed out.

"You don't look like a man who would have the guts to kill another man," said Hank. "How many have you killed?"

"Some!" replied Brogan.

"And you say you're not a wanted man?"

"Nope! Anyone I've killed have deserved it an' it was all legal like. Not like you."

Hank studied Brogan for a few moments, noting the cool steeliness of his eyes and calm manner. "Yeh, I guess I can believe you have killed a few men. Here's a word of warnin' though. If we should ever meet up again, don't expect no quarter from me. I told you I'm fast with this gun an' very accurate."

"I'll try to remember that," said Brogan. "Now, if you don't mind I'll be on my way. Like I said, you just keep on walkin' for that mountain an' you should be clear within three days."

Brogan collected his belongings together and stowed them away in his saddle-bags, all the time keeping a wary eye on Hank. Hank sensed that he was under careful scrutiny and, although he was very tempted, he made no effort to tackle the saddle tramp. It was not that he felt intimidated, but he sensed that the saddle tramp was not a man to be so easily taken.

"An' what do I do for food in those three days?" he asked.

"There's plenty of snakes an' lizards," said Brogan. "Snakes is the easiest to catch. The best part of lizards is the tail. You oughta be able to find enough to see you through. If you can't find any water, chewin' on cactus'll give you enough water so's you won't die of thirst. Don't try swallowin' it though, all that'll do is give you stomach ache. Just chew it until there ain't no more water left then spit it out."

"Thanks for the tips," said Hank. "I hope I can return the favour some day." He laughed sarcastically.

"Don't need no favours from nobody," Brogan grunted, mounting his old horse. "Me an' my old girl here gets by without favours, don't we?" He patted her neck and she nodded her head in seeming agreement. "'Sides, with luck I'll never clap eyes on you again, not that I've got anythin' personal against

18

you, 'ceptin' you admitted you might've killed me, it's just that I ain't one for chewin' over the fat of old times with nobody."

"I suppose I oughta be grateful for you not decidin' to take me to the law," said Hank. "Strange thing is, I'm not. Maybe if we do meet up again you might wish you'd either killed me or taken me in."

"Maybe so," agreed Brogan. "I ain't perfect. It's a chance I'll just have to take."

"I could kill you as you ride out," Hank pointed out.

"You could try," agreed Brogan, "but you'll either be dead yourself or I'll be out of range. That gun of yours is an old Adams, anythin' over twenty yards an' they're useless . . . " He patted his holster. "This Colt on the other hand's got a range of at least another ten yards. You oughta know that if you is the shootin' champion you claim you are."

Hank was only too well aware of the

19

limitations of his Adams and, since he had no rifle, he knew it would be extremely stupid of him to attempt to take the saddle tramp who was even now at the extreme limit of the range of his Adams.

Hank kept in full view of the steadily disappearing Brogan until rider and horse disappeared from view. He cursed himself for the way things had turned out, for being caught out by such an old trick and at the same time wondered if Brogan had really heard him as easily as he claimed he had. He decided to believe the saddle tramp; he was not stupid; he realized that he was a greenhorn from the city and had a lot to learn about the ways of the west.

"Reckon you'll see him again?" Brogan asked himself.

"Wouldn't be surprised," he admitted. He often talked to himself or his horse. Usually he got more sense out the horse. "Depends on what he does next an' which way he's headed."

"Maybe we shoulda let him ride with

us," he addressed this remark to his horse who shook her head violently. "No? Yeh, maybe you is right. Still feel kinda guilty though, young city feller tacklin' the desert on his own."

"Guilty?" he exclaimed. "He said himself he might've killed us. What the hell you got to feel guilty about? You told him what to eat an' how to get water, what more could you do?"

"Not a lot, I guess. OK, all we gotta do is get across this lot an' find some decent drinkin' water an' some supplies."

Satisfied with his conversation with himself and his horse, he allowed her to plod on at her own pace. He had nowhere in particular to go and no particular time in which to do it.

★ ★ ★

Hank Carter started walking towards the mountain Brogan had indicated. After more than three hours walking the peak seemed further away than ever and it was the sight of a large rattlesnake alongside a clear water-hole that persuaded him to stop for the night.

It took two shots to kill the snake, despite his claim to be a champion shot and, once it was dead and he had performed the messy task of skinning it, he was then faced with the task of cooking it. With no means of lighting a fire, he had to rely on tales he had heard about lighting a fire by rubbing two dry sticks together.

He did manage to find enough dry scrub, but finding two suitable sticks proved harder than expected. His first two attempts ended in failure as the sticks simply shattered. It took him another two hours before he was able to get his fire going, but by that time, when he eventually turned back to his snake, he found it covered in flies and bugs. He had not seen a fly for two weeks and suddenly the whole place seemed to be swarming with them.

"Hell! Didn't fancy no more snake

anyhow!" He threw the offending, bug-ridden piece of meat as far as he could. After a very short time the flies too disappeared. However, as the night closed in he was very grateful for that fire; it seemed a lot colder than it had on previous nights.

"Damn you, McNally!" he swore. "Leavin' me here like this. You'd better just hope we don't meet up again!"

2

THERE did not seem to be any way of avoiding it. Either side of the narrow pass rose in sheer cliffs, varying between about thirty and a hundred feet in height and stretching as far as the eye could see. Scaling them looked impossible, especially with a horse and it was not normally something that either Brogan or his ageing horse would attempt.

There seemed to be no alternative but to go through the pass. That in itself was not the problem, the problem presented itself in the form of what appeared to be a trading post in the entrance.

Brogan had a thing against trading posts, especially in this part of the world. He had generally found them to be the hangout of outlaws and other unsavoury characters he liked to avoid. It was not that he was scared of any of them, it was simply that he had found there was always someone who, for whatever reason, wanted to challenge him. There was always one who disliked his appearance, his mode of life or even the way he talked.

As for the 'unsavoury' characters, he had to admit that he hardly qualified as the most savoury or respectable of people but, despite his admittedly 'nosey' nature, he always tried to avoid confrontation wherever possible.

Through his spyglass he had decided that the half-dozen men lounging outside the single-storey building were decidedly unsavoury and probably spelled trouble. However, apart from returning across the desert, there seemed to be nothing else he could do but ride on through. Ride on through was exactly what he intended to do. Although he was in need of supplies he would not get them from this particular post. Quite apart from the probability of trouble, the prices he would be charged would be at least double those in a general store in any town.

"OK, old girl," he muttered, patting the neck of his horse, just keep on goin' an' hope for the best." She nodded her head in agreement and slowly plodded forward.

The men at the post seemed to show little interest in his approach, apart from one who disappeared inside the building, but Brogan knew that he was being carefully studied and assessed to see if he had anything worth stealing. Apart from his guns, a Colt and a Winchester rifle, some eighty dollars carefully lined in the soles of his boots, the sum total of Brogan's worth was precisely zero and most people knew it.

It was not until it became obvious that he was not going to stop that any other interest was taken in him. He was more or less forced to stop when he detected the cocking of various guns and the command of a gruff voice.

"Not so fast, stranger!" came the

command. "You got somethin' against Luke Harman?"

"Nope!" replied Brogan. "I ain't never heard of Luke Harman."

"That's his name over the store," said the man, the biggest man in the group.

"Yeh, I seen that," agreed Brogan.

Indeed, the name over the store did make it plain that this was LUKE HARMAN'S TRADING POST and Brogan wondered if the man questioning him was *the* Luke Harman.

"He don't like it when folk don't do no trade with him," sneered the big man, walking towards Brogan. "It ain't friendly an' it sure ain't good for trade. Why, if everyone was like you an' simply rode past the store might as well close up."

"If everyone was like me," said Brogan, smiling slightly, "Luke Harman's Tradin' Post would've closed long ago."

"What you mean by that?" The big man seemed mystified.

"How many saddle tramps you know got any money?" replied Brogan.

The big man studied Brogan for a few moments and then cast his eye over the horse. "Yeh, see what you mean; no self-respectin' traveller would be seen dead on a nag like that. So, you're a saddle tramp? Strange that, you're the first one I ever met what admitted to it, most claim they're just driftin' through lookin' for work."

"Work!" Brogan laughed loudly. "Mister, I ain't never done no work since I was a boy, an' even then I don't recall doin' that much. Yeh, I'm a saddle tramp an' proud of it. I mind my own business an don't bother nobody."

"'Ceptin' steal what you want!" Brogan chose to ignore the remark and just smiled. "OK, on your way, but I'd steer clear of Appleby if I was you."

"Appleby?" Brogan asked.

"Yeh, it's about thirty miles due west. Small town but a real mean sheriff; he don't like saddle bums, drifters an' outlaws, in that order."

"That why you is all holin' up out here?" Brogan could not resist goading the big man slightly.

"Somethin' like that," came the reply, missing the goad put out by Brogan.

"Thanks for the warnin'," said Brogan, really quite appreciative of the information. "Maybe I'll give Appleby a miss." He started forward and then stopped and looked back. "Could be you'll be gettin' another stranger comin' through in the next couple of days. He won't be on a horse though, he'll be walkin': his horse died under him about two weeks ago. I gave him some food out there an pointed him in this direction. Name of Hank Carter; young feller, early twenties I'd say. Don't know what he's got in the way of money, but he'll sure be footsore an' hungry."

"You left a man out there?" exclaimed the big man.

"He warn't in no danger," assured Brogan. "'Sides, he was goin' to kill me just for my horse an I don't take too kindly to things like that."

The big man laughed loudly. "Can't say as I would too. OK, we'll be on the lookout for him. What you say his name was?"

"Carter, Hank Carter, greenhorn city feller lookin' to make it good out here."

The big man laughed again. "I reckon we might just be able to help him!"

Brogan was not sure if Hank Carter was going to appreciate the help he was liable to receive but he was not concerned, it was Hank's business, not his.

★ ★ ★

It would have been quite easy to avoid the town of Appleby, but two things finally decided Brogan that he needed to go there. One was his lack of supplies and the second was that his horse had developed a lame foot.

For the moment the lameness did not seem too bad, but an examination showed that it was liable to get worse. There appeared to be an abscess forming and medication and treatment by a veterinarian was the best course of action.

Brogan had treated an abscess on his horse once before, but that was many years ago when both he and horse were much younger. To perform the operation himself now could well lead to complications, complications such as the death of the animal. Quite apart from not wishing to do away with her, he could hardly afford to purchase another horse.

The big man at the trading post had been right when he said that the sheriff of Appleby did not like saddle tramps. Brogan had hardly been in the small town five minutes before he was approached by a tall, thin and very aggressive man wearing a badge which proclaimed him to be the sheriff.

"Hope you don't intend stoppin'!" barked the sheriff as Brogan dismounted and picked up the damaged forehoof of his horse to check it. "We don't like saddle bums or drifters in this town."

"So I been told," muttered Brogan.

"Told! Who told you?" demanded the sheriff.

"Some feller out at Harman's Tradin' Post," replied Brogan.

"Scum!" retorted the sheriff, spitting venomously on the ground.

"Can't say as I disagree with that," conceded Brogan. He stood up and looked the sheriff squarely in the face, surprised to find that he was in fact slightly the taller. It was the sheriffs extremely thin build which gave the illusion of height. "What makes you think I'm a saddle tramp? I could be lookin' for work."

The sheriff was unused to people like Brogan staring him out and bowed his head slightly to avert Brogan's steely eyes. "You got it written all over you!"

he asserted. "I'd say you ain't never done no work in your life."

Brogan smiled slightly. Normally he would have conducted his business and left town but, just occasionally, he could not resist the desire to goad sheriffs like this one. Now he had another reason for staying, the damage to his horse.

"Can't expect a man to ride out with a lame horse." He pointed at the offending hoof which showed quite plain signs of the abscess. "Even if you don't like me, you got no cause to make the horse suffer."

The sheriff bent down to examine the hoof and eventually stood and grunted. "Best get Doc Vernon to look at it, he's the animal doctor. If he says the horse can be ridden you just make sure you're ridin' it out within one minute of him sayin' so."

"An' if he says she can't be ridden?" prompted Brogan.

The sheriff grunted again. "We'll see! Right now I'm gonna look through my files an' find out just what you're wanted for."

"You'd be wastin' your time," assured Brogan. "Saddle tramp I may be, but I ain't wanted by nobody for nothin' nowheres!"

"Seems to me I heard that before!" sneered the sheriff. "I'll be lookin' all the same. What you say your name was?"

"I didn't," replied Brogan. "You never asked."

"Well I'm askin' now, smart arse!"

"OK, it's McNally, Brogan Mc-Nally . . . "

"Don't suppose that's your real name."

"You reckon I made up the name 'Brogan'?"

"Yeh . . . well, maybe it is your given name; I'll be checkin' just the same."

"Seems to me you'd be better used roundin' up them layabouts out at Harman's Tradin' Post," said Brogan. "I reckon every one of 'em must have a price."

"Sure, every damned one of 'em!" snarled the sheriff. "Only trouble is I can't touch any one of 'em just so long as they stay that end of the pass."

"Why the hell not?"

"A little matter of that's where the State border is," grumbled the sheriff. "The tradin' post is half a mile the other side of the border. They can sit there all year long an' there ain't a thing I can do about it."

"So why don't the sheriff from over the border do somethin'?"

The sheriff laughed loudly. "McNally, you just come through there; you must've ridden across the desert. What sheriff in his right mind is gonna bother about a bunch of hoodlums holed up in some rat-infested tradin' post on the edge of his territory, especially when it means a couple of days crossin' that desert? I know damned well it wouldn't bother me."

"You've got a point," admitted Brogan. "An' they is far enough

35

away not to bother you too much I suppose."

"They know the score," grunted the sheriff. "They leave my territory alone an' I leave them alone."

"Seems like Hank Carter is headin' for good company," Brogan observed.

"Hank Carter?" The sheriff seemed interested. "What do you know about Hank Carter?"

"Nothin' 'ceptin' he's headed this way," said Brogan. "I left him walkin' across the desert."

The sheriff pulled a folded wanted poster out of his pocket and showed it to Brogan. "Don't expect you to be able read what it says," he said, "but you've seen him, is that a good picture?"

"Wanted for the murder of Judge Michael Short, Jeremy Short and Michael Short Junior, both sons of Judge Michael Short. $1000 dollars dead an' $2000 dollars alive," Brogan read, whistling slightly. "Last poster I seen the price was only seven fifty an' five hundred. What happened?"

"I reckon the judge's family must've put the extra money up." He looked hard at Brogan. "You knew who he was an' what he was wanted for? Why didn't you bring him in?"

"I ain't no bounty hunter," replied Brogan. "I'm rather like you an' the men out at the tradin' post, they leave me alone, I leave them alone."

The sheriff grunted. "Useful money for the likes of you though. Makes a change to find a saddle bum what can read."

"Strange as it may seem, Sheriff, I ain't that interested in money. Just so long as I've got me enough for my needs I don't want no more an as for readin', I decided when I was a boy that readin' an' writin' were the two things I had to learn."

"OK, I'm convinced," muttered the sheriff. "You probably ain't got no wanted poster out on you, but it still stands, what I said about Doc Vernon an your horse. The doc's place is down the street . . . " He pointed in the direction of the small but clean and neat church at the end of the street. "Turn up by the church an' his place is the second house; can't miss it, there's only two of 'em an' the first belongs to Doc Cunliffe; he's the regular people doctor. Mind, if you want a tooth pulled Doc Vernon is better at it than Doc Cunliffe."

"My teeth are fine!" grinned Brogan. "OK, see you later, Sheriff." He led his horse down the street and easily found Doc Vernon.

The veterinarian confirmed that it would do irreparable damage if the horse was to be ridden for at least a week and Brogan obtained an assurance from the veterinarian that the sheriff would be informed.

"I'd still make yourself scarce though," advised Doc Vernon. "Sheriff Weaver don't like to see saddle tramps or layabouts in town, an' that goes for most the townsfolk too. You just keep your head down an' mind your own business an everythin' should be fine. I reckon you're goin' to have trouble findin' a place to stay though . . . " He looked Brogan up and down critically. "Maybe if you had a bath it might help."

Brogan laughed. "Don't worry 'bout where I'm gonna stay, Doc. Me an' beds ain't too happy together. I been sleepin' on the bare ground for so long now I can't take to a soft bed. I'll see if I can sleep in the livery alongside my horse, that's what I usually end up doin'."

"I reckon you could still do with a bath though," said the doc, sniffing slightly and wrinkling his nose. "You smell bad enough to scare a skunk. They got baths at the barber's shop . . . "

"Bathin' ain't healthy!" interrupted Brogan, fiercely. He always objected most strongly when it was suggested he take to soap and hot water. "I had me two baths in hot water with real soap in the past two years an' I caught me one hell of humdinger of

a cold after each one. No, sir, bathin'
ain't healthy!"

Doc Vernon laughed lightly. "In your
case you are probably right, it'd be too
much of a shock to the system. Pete
at the livery is fairly accommodatin', I
don't suppose he'll have any objection
to you sleepin' there, that is if the horses
don't mind . . . " He laughed at his
own joke, but Brogan had heard it all
before — many times. "Talkin' about
accommodation, that costs money an'
so does tendin' your horse . . . "

"How much, Doc?" Brogan sighed,
pulling off his boot, much to the
amazement of the veterinarian who
was unsure if the colour of Brogan's
feet was caused by wearing socks or
ingrained dirt. In the event it proved
to be the colour of Brogan's socks.

"Er . . . four dollars," said the
veterinarian. "Includin' some powder
you've got to put on that hoof . . . "
He reached on to a shelf and took down
a package. "Just sprinkle this all over
it twice a day, night an' mornin'. If it

ain't no better by the end of the week bring her back an' I'll see what else I can do. It should be all right though, I've drained all the puss."

Brogan handed the doc a grubby ten-dollar bill and waited for the change before putting his boot on again. The veterinarian handled the note as though it would suddenly curl up and bite him.

Pete, the owner of the livery stable, was quite happy to take both Brogan and his horse at a charge of one dollar a day for the horse, including feed, and fifty cents a night for Brogan.

"You gotta find your own feed though!" Pete joked.

Brogan considered fifty cents rather a hefty charge for doing nothing but sleep on hay and after a bit of haggling Pete finally agreed on a dollar for the duration of Brogan's stay, whether it was for one night or seven — in advance. Satisfied with the deal and that his horse was properly fed, Brogan wandered down the street to the one and only saloon, which proved to be completely empty.

"Busy place!" Brogan observed as he leaned on the counter. "Beer, if you don't mind."

"Beer it is," muttered the bartender. "Folk round here don't start their drinkin' until after eight, 'ceptin' on a Friday an' Saturday. Sunday I don't open at all; it just ain't worth the bother.

"I can imagine," said Brogan. "I've kinda lost track of days, what day is it today?"

"Monday, worst day of the week barrin' Sunday."

"You should get some girls, that'd bring the customers in," advised Brogan.

"Tried that once," the bartender said, smiling weakly. "They'd all been run out of town in less'n a week."

"By the men?"

"Naw, leastways not most of 'em, although the preacher did manage to get a few with him. It was the women; they just ganged up and hustled the girls out; they even paid their fares to Denver."

The saloon may not have been able to offer much in the way of entertainment, although Brogan was not really looking for anything like that, but it did provide just about the best beer he had ever tasted.

Just before eight o'clock Sheriff Weaver came into the saloon, apparently looking for Brogan. He refused the offer of a drink.

"I want you out of here in two minutes!" Weaver ordered. "This is about the time decent folk start comin' in. Folk in these parts are very particular who they drink with."

"Has Doc Vernon told you about my horse?" asked Brogan with a grin. "He reckons I can't ride her for at least a week."

"He told me!" confirmed Weaver. "OK, I'm a man of my word, you can stay until she's fit, but not a moment longer. In the meantime I mean what I say when I tell you to get your butt out of this saloon."

"You denyin' a feller a drink?"

"I ain't denyin' you nothin'," grated the sheriff. He looked at the bartender. "How many has he had?"

"Two beers," replied the bartender, which was correct.

"Well now," grinned the sheriff. "I'd say that was enough to make you drunk, wouldn't you, Sam?" The bartender nodded.

"Two beers!" exclaimed Brogan. "Two beers hardly wets the back of a man's throat."

"Not Sam's beer," assured Weaver. Brogan had to admit that it did seem stronger than any other he had tasted. "Two beers is more than any normal man can take. Now, you've got two choices McNally: you can do like I say an' get out of here right now, an' don't come back tonight, or you can spend the night in jail." He sniffed the air. "Personally I'd prefer it if I didn't have to hold you for the night. Choice is yours."

"You just convinced me I've had enough," said Brogan, grinning. "One thing I like about this town is it's so friendly. OK, I'm used to turnin' in at sunset anyhow, so I'm already up later than usual. I expect I'll be seein' you in the mornin'. Is there anywhere I shouldn't go? I've gotta eat sometime an' I ain't eaten since this mornin'."

"I guess I can't deny you a meal," Weaver grunted. "Only place there is that's likely to serve you is Bess Pringle's place, she ain't too particular."

Brogan laughed. He had the feeling that he had met the likes of Bess Pringle before. He did not argue and went along to the eating house at the opposite end of the town to the church where, as expected, he had met Bess Pringle before, or at least he had met Bess Pringles in other towns.

This one was no different to the others, bemoaning the stuck-up women of the town and making not very subtle hints that she provided other services than food. Like all the other

45

Bess Pringles he had met, she was an excellent cook and very cheap. He ate his food, told her that he would be in for breakfast in the morning at about eight, declined her offer of a bed for the night and returned to the livery stable. He wondered if he would be able to hold back the advances of Bess Pringle for a whole week. Even he had his breaking point and weaknesses and one thing that did attract him to her was the fact that she never mentioned soap and water.

3

HANK CARTER almost cried with relief when he saw the trading post coolly sheltering in the shade of the cliff. His boots had long since been cast aside since it had become harder to walk in them than without them. However, the price had been paid in swollen and torn feet. He just about managed to stagger into the cool of the store, idly watched by the same men who had seen Brogan ride by but who made no move to help.

"You must be Hank Carter," one of the men said casually when Hank had managed to recover somewhat.

"How the hell do you know my name?" Hank wheezed.

"Some saddle tramp passin' through a couple of days ago told us you might be comin'." His concern for the condition of Hank seemed almost non-existent.

"I would've thought one of you would have offered me some water," gasped Hank. "I've just had to walk God knows how many miles across that desert."

"Fifty cents!" the man said, smiling broadly.

"Fifty . . . I don't believe it! A man has just spent three weeks in the desert and is almost dead from exhaustion and thirst and you want to charge him for some water . . . "

"Water ain't cheap," replied the man, completely unconcerned. "You want water, we got water, but water in these parts is scarcer'n whisky. One mug of water is fifty cents, take it or leave it, I don't care much either way."

"Bastard!" oathed Hank. "OK, OK. . . . " He reached groggily into his hip pocket and pulled out a silver dollar. "Better make that two, I'm goin' to need them."

Hank wondered why another man, small, dirty and unshaven with a distinct twist to his mouth, was looking at him so intently. What he did not realize was that in taking the silver dollar out of his hip pocket he had also pulled out a large wad of notes, all the money he possessed and amounting to something over $3,000. The small twisted mouth twitched in anticipation as even his uneducated mind calculated at least $2,000. It appeared that none of the others had seen the wad. As Hank moved he felt the money against his hip and, realizing what had happened, quickly returned it to his pocket. He now knew why the man had been so interested in him.

A large mug of water was produced and the silver dollar quickly pocketed. Hank drank the cool liquid slowly, savouring every soothing drop as it coursed down his dry throat. The second mug was produced as soon as he had finished the first, but this time Hank was content to simply pour it over his dry, dusty face.

"That's better!" he sighed, shaking

his head. "That was a dollar well spent."

"I'd say it was mighty expensive water!"

Hank blinked his eyes and found himself staring into the barrel of a gun. His eyes slowly followed the line of the gun and the arm and hand holding it until he was staring into the twisted mouth of the small thin man.

"Should've guessed!" Hank muttered.

"Should've been more careful!" hissed Twisted Mouth. "Hand over that roll you got tucked in your back pocket an' you won't get hurt!"

Hank looked about at the others, only two of whom were witness to what was happening, who simply smiled and did nothing. He muttered something and shuffled slightly, making a bit more of a show about it than was really necessary, but none of them seemed to notice. Hank's hand slipped to his side . . .

The single shot brought the others dashing into the store, guns drawn and ready. Twisted Mouth lay sprawled across the wooden floor, his twisted lips obliterated by a gaping hole where the bullet from Hank's Adams had blasted through. The man's legs and hands twitched for a few seconds before the life finally drained away from the small, dirty body.

Hank looked up into seven guns all aimed steadily at him and braced himself for the expected thud of bullets. He relaxed slightly when, after about thirty seconds, he was still alive and uninjured.

"Stupid bastard!" muttered the biggest of the men. "Never had a lick of sense in his body. Just what the hell was all that about anyhow?" He addressed the man who apparently owned the trading post.

"Don't rightly know," replied the man, Luke Harman. "All I know is Rosie pulled his gun on this feller."

"What he do that for?" demanded the big man.

"I haven't the faintest idea," lied

Hank, fairly certain that none of the others knew about his money.

"I haven't the faintest idea!" mimicked the big man in what he thought was an eastern accent. "Come off it, Mister, even Rosie don't go pullin' a gun on someone for no reason at all."

"Well there was no reason as far as I'm concerned!" muttered Hank, finding new energies and struggling to his feet. It seemed that none of them was going to take undue exception to the death of Rosie, a fact confirmed when they all put their guns away.

"There's a hundred dollars reward if you take his body into Appleby," said one of the others. "Would've been two hundred if he'd still been alive."

"You take him!" muttered Hank. "Right now I got me more important things to do, like buy me a new pair of boots!"

"Ain't no use in any of us takin' him in," sighed the big man. "We is all worth more'n Rosie; we'd never get out of there."

"So you're all worth money, why doesn't the sheriff or the constable or whatever he is come out here and get you?" asked Hank.

"Ah well," said one of the others, with a distinct Irish accent. "It's all a matter of territory, see . . . " Hank did not see. "It's like this," Irish continued. "Where we are right now is in one State and where the sheriff is is in another. That means he can't come and get us, but we can't go to him either but the sheriff who covers this part of this State doesn't want to know about comin' out here after us so, as long as we stay here, we're safe."

"Nice set up," agreed Hank. "Maybe I'd better stay here a while until things cool down."

"The law's after you as well then?" said Irish. "We thought it might be. Sure, this is as good a place as any; that's how come we are all here, we just sort of drifted in in ones and twos."

"What you do?" asked the big man, whose name proved to be nothing more original than 'Bull'.

"Killed a judge and his two sons," said Hank, casually.

"Killed a ju . . . " exclaimed Bull. "Hell, that's bad news man, real bad news. They know you is headed this way?"

"I suppose so," admitted Hank. "I know they were following me just over three weeks ago. I've not seen anythin' of them since I entered the desert."

Irish sighed heavily and sadly shook his head. "Just when I thought I might be gettin' a bit of peace in me old age . . . One thing you can be quite certain of, Mr Carter, is that even now there's someone out there lookin' for you. If it'd just been some other man who was nobody you'd killed, they would probably have given up by now, but a judge . . . I think the best thing all of us can do is ride out of here right now. If they take you they'll be takin' all of us, nothin' more certain; we'd be a bonus for them."

"Irish is right!" muttered Bull. "Kill

a farmer or a cowboy an' they soon forget, but if it happens to be one of their own, sheriff, marshal or judge, then you got trouble, they all close ranks an' there ain't nowheres you is gonna hide an' State boundaries don't mean a thing."

Hank looked at them all in slight disbelief, but he could tell from their expressions that they at least believed every word of what they were saying. He had to admit that he was inclined to believe it as well. The law had already followed him from the east coast to more than two-thirds the way across America, so it seemed highly unlikely that they would abandon their pursuit now.

"Then I guess I'll just have to move on," Hank said eventually. "First though I need me some new boots, new clothes and a horse. I could do with a rifle too if you've got one."

"Seems to me you just laid claim to a horse an' a rifle," said Bull. "You just killed Rosie so I guess that gives you claim to what was his. That's the way things go out here," he said in response to the slightly puzzled look on Hank's face.

Hank grunted. "Guess so!" He looked at the small, twisted form still lying on the floor and now attracting numerous flies. "His clothes are no use to me though, he was a lot smaller'n me."

"There's boots an' clothes over on them shelves," said Harman, indicating some dusty shelves at the back of the store. "There's sure to be somethin' your size; I get bigger men than you passin' through."

Hank went across to the shelves and eventually sorted himself out two shirts, two pairs of jeans, discarding his own, tattered shirt and jeans and wearing the new ones, a pair of socks and a pair of boots. He had been going to buy a jacket, but they were all either far too big or too small, so he did not bother.

"Twenty-five dollars!" said Harman

after seeing what Hank had chosen.

"Twenty-five!" exclaimed Hank. "I could get the lot for ten back east."

"Then you just go back east an' get 'em," invited Harman. "Twenty-five it is, not one cent less."

Hank grumbled but agreed, pulling the wad of money from his discarded jeans, trying to hide the fact, but he knew very well that he had not. He handed Harman thirty dollars and waited while the trader had to hunt for five dollars in change.

The next thing Hank did was to take up the offer of food which, though plain and badly cooked as it was and for which he was charged one dollar, tasted like pure nectar after his three weeks of wandering. Over his meal he had chance to talk with the others.

"So what is you gonna do now?" asked Bull.

"It seems I haven't got much option but to move on," said Hank. "What's up ahead?"

"Appleby; that's about thirty miles,"

said Bull. "Other than that, the next town I know is maybe a hundred miles."

"I reckon Appleby could be avoided," said Hank. "What are you goin' to do, sit here and chance the posse followin' me?"

"Could do I suppose, but I don't fancy the idea. I did that once before and got arrested for my trouble. Luke's OK; he owns this place an' he ain't wanted for nothin', leastwise he reckons he ain't. Ain't that so, Luke?"

"I ain't!" assured Harman.

"Then I guess the rest of us is just gonna have to get the hell out of here for a while," continued Bull. "Maybe we'll come back when it all cools down, whenever that's gonna be."

"Ain't no need to rush yourselves," Harman sneered. "I managed without you before you came an' I reckon I can manage fine without you after you've all gone. None of you ain't never spent nothin' with me anyhow."

"Maybe that's 'cos you ain't got

nothin' worth buyin'!" sneered one of the others.

"Where will you go?" asked Hank. "I'm a stranger here: I've never been away from the east before."

"And why should you be wantin' to know that?" asked Irish.

"I was thinkin' that maybe I'll go with you," said Hank. "I'm wanted too, remember."

"We remember!" said Irish. "If it wasn't for you we wouldn't be havin' to think about leavin' now, would we!"

Hank sat thoughtfully for a while. "We'd probably stand a better chance if we did team up together. At least we can give each other some sort of protection."

They all looked at each other for a few minutes, mulling over the implications of forming a band. Hank detected a slight nod from Irish and Bull and two of the others, but the other two were shaking their heads.

"Not me!" said one by the name of Billy Clayton who was shaking his head.

"I don't reckon either me or Jim . . . "
— Jim was the other man shaking his head — "wanna get involved. I reckon we'll just ride out of here by ourselves."

"I'm for it," said Bull. "How about you, Irish?"

"Well now," said Irish. "I never was one for bein' on me own. I'm not all that bright when it comes to thinkin', but I'm not all that sure it would be wise."

"Have you a better idea?" asked Hank.

"No, to be honest I have not," Irish sighed. "I only said I wasn't sure it would be wise, but since I'm not even sure what that means, I guess I'm with you. OK, you've convinced me. How about you two?" He addressed the other two men who were called Slim Jones and Eli Smith. At least they were the names they admitted to but everyone was quite certain they were not their real names.

"Might as well," agreed Slim.

"Yeh, me too," nodded Eli. "One condition though: if any of us wanna split at any time he's free to if he wants."

"Yeh," nodded Bill. "That goes for me too."

"I don't see any problem there," agreed Hank.

"There is just one more point," said Irish. "Maybe I don't think too good, but it strikes me that folk like us are not goin' to come by money too easy or too legal like, we'll have to take what we can when we can . . . "

There was a murmur of agreement. "That means that if any of us does decide to split, he takes with him his fair share of whatever there is to take an' no arguin'."

Hank looked at the others who nodded in agreement. "That seems only fair," he said. "Now, in any group there's always one who has to give orders . . . I mean make decisions. Now I don't know this country and I don't know that much about the folk

61

who live here . . . "

"You've got the job!" said Bull. "But only on account you must've done schoolin' which is more than any of us have, so you is the best man for the job. Agreed?" He asked the others.

"Reckon so!" They nodded.

"You two still for goin' out on your own?" Hank asked Billy and Jim. "I reckon you'd stand a better chance with us."

Jim looked at his companion, who shook his head. "Naw, we go by ourselves."

"Sorry to hear it," said Hank as the pair stood up and made their way to the door. "Best of luck. Which way are you goin'?"

"That's our business!" muttered Billy. "What you don't know can't hurt us. As far as we're concerned you spell nothin' but trouble, Carter."

"You mean you're not in enough trouble already?" Hank sneered.

"Compared to the kinda trouble you

is an' what you is headin' for, we is small fry," muttered Billy. "You just mind what I say," he addressed the others. "Only thing that can happen to you by teamin' up with a judge-killer is endin' up dead."

Billy and Jim stomped out of the store and could be heard preparing their horses.

"Take no heed of them," said Eli. "Billy is sore 'cos you killed Rosie. Rosie was his buddy."

Rosie's body had been removed from the store, but had simply been left outside, where even more flies had descended on it.

"Yeh," said Hank. "Well then, maybe it's as well he isn't with us; he might just decide to put a bullet in the back of my head if he was. OK, that's settled then. The question now is what do we do now or, more importantly, which way do we go? Like I say, I don't know the territory, so it's up to you."

"I'm thinkin' that we don't have that

much choice," said Irish. "There's sure to be a posse or somebody lookin' for you, so ridin' back through the desert is askin' for trouble."

"For a man who reckons he ain't too good at thinkin', you sure seem to do a lot of it!" laughed Bull.

"That's just me way of thinkin'," Irish grinned.

Hank had already decided that the Irishman was not quite so simple as he made out and was probably a good man to have on his side.

"We could go either north or south," suggested Slim.

"Naw!" grunted Bull. "North is nothin' but more desert for two or three hundred miles an' no waterin' places — I know, I've done it a couple of times. South you come to a canyon an' there just ain't no way round for at least a hundred miles.

"Then it looks like we've got no choice but to head west," said Hank. "Only trouble with that is it takes us to that sheriff you were talkin' about."

"Weaver!" Bull muttered. "Thin as a piece of grass but a real mean feller."

"There'd be five of us," Hank pointed out. "I don't think he would dare tackle five of us."

"Maybe not on his own," agreed Bull, "but if he tells the town of Appleby to jump even the houses ask 'How high?'."

"The thing is," said Hank, "he won't be expectin' us."

"There ain't no need to go into Appleby at all," Slim pointed out. "It's the best part of thirty miles from here. Once we're through the pass we can head which ever way we want."

"And go where?" asked Hank. "We can't avoid every town we come to, can we?"

"Guess not," agreed Slim, "but it might be a good idea to put as much distance between a place like Appleby, where we is known, an' head for somewheres we ain't known."

"You can bet your life there's posters

up for you all over the place," said Hank.

"Don't know about us," said Eli, "but there's sure to be your poster everywhere."

Hank shrugged. Actually he was quite enjoying his apparent notoriety. "What kind of town is Appleby?"

"Usual," said Bull. "Ranchin' an' farmin' mainly. There's a couple of small gold mines, but not much else. As far as towns go out here, it's probably better off than most. Nothin' to compare with anythin' you got back east though."

"Yeh, towns out here hardly qualify for bein' called a village where I come from," said Hank. "Still, that's the way things are. I suppose it's got a bank."

"Sure it has," said Irish. "I was in there once and it seemed a very busy place."

"You were in a bank?" laughed Eli. "What the hell were you in there for, tryin' to rob the place?"

"I was givin' the matter serious

consideration," said Irish, solemnly. "Me and the man I was with finally decided that it couldn't be done, not by the two of us anyhow."

"What happened to him?" asked Hank.

"Got bitten by a rattlesnake," said Irish, laughing slightly. "I told him to watch, it wasn't dead, but he didn't believe me. He's buried up there somewhere now." He nodded behind him.

"Talkin' about buryin'," said Harman. "There's a body out there gotta be got rid of. If he's left much longer he'll be stinkin' the place out."

"Then you won't notice the smell!" laughed Bull.

"He's right though," said Hank, laughing as well. "We'd better dig a hole for him."

"You mean we'll dig the hole," said Irish. "Since you've been appointed our leader, I don't suppose you include yourself in that."

"It doesn't need five of us to dig a

hole," said Hank. "You and Slim can do it."

"See what I mean!" said Irish, shrugging.

"He can wait a while longer," said Hank. "I'm interested in this bank in Appleby. Tell me all you know about it."

"There's a man here what knows better than anyone," said Irish. "Luke must've been in there lots of times.

"You figurin' on robbin' that bank?" asked Eli.

"Why not?" said Hank. "If you want to go on runnin' from the law all your life and showin' nothin' for it, that's fine. Personally I don't intend to. I want to find me somewhere to settle down, some place I'm not known or can't be got at and for that I need cash."

"Seems to me you got all the cash you need," said Bull.

"That's the difference between you and me," sneered Hank. "To you a couple of thousand seems like a fortune. I'm talkin' about real money, ten maybe twenty thousand."

"Sure could have a helluva time with a couple of thousand though," said Eli.

"How old are you, Eli?" asked Hank.

"Old?" Eli looked mystified. "I ain't sure. I reckon I'm about forty-five, maybe fifty. What you wanna know for?"

"How many of those years have you been runnin' from the law?"

"Apart from four years in the pen, I suppose since I was about fifteen when my pa threw me out. Why?"

"So let's say you've been avoiding the law for thirty years. Wouldn't you like to settle down?"

"Reckon so," Eli agreed.

"I'm just twenty-six," said Hank. "I've only been on the run for about three months and I don't intend to make it thirty years. My idea is to pull a couple of good bank robberies and then get the hell out of it to either Canada or Mexico and buy me a ranch or a farm or somethin'."

"Canada or Mexico?" said Irish. "Won't the law still come after you there?"

"No," Hank assured. "Just so long as you don't do nothin' against the law in that country there's nothin' neither they nor the law here can do."

"A farm!" Irish sighed. "When I was a boy in Ireland I lived on a farm. I thought it was damned hard work then, that's why I skipped out an' came here. Things didn't work out though an' now look at the mess I'm in."

"You'd like a farm again?" asked Hank.

"Seems like a dream!" Irish sighed.

"But it's a dream that can happen!" said Hank. "Two, maybe three good banks, a quick run for the border and you can have your farm."

"An' you is thinkin' that maybe Appleby is a good place to start?" said Slim.

"I don't know anythin' about the place," said Hank, "but it sounds like a fair place to start."

"You oughta know!" Bull turned to Luke Harman. "You got any idea what kinda money they carry in the bank?"

"Rather like shittin' on my own doorstep!" muttered Harman. "It ain't a bad bank, not the biggest, but I reckon there must be somethin' like twenty thousand dollars in there at any one time. There's more at the end of every month when the farmers an' ranchers draw wages for their hands an' pay their bills."

"What day is it now?" asked Slim.

Hank consulted a pocket book and did a mental calculation. "I think it must be the 27th. Wednesday the 27th. Pay days are usually on a Saturday. How does the extra cash arrive?"

"One thing Appleby has got is a railroad runnin' through," said Harman. "Things mostly go in an' out by train."

"OK, so let's suppose that the extra money comes in on Friday, that's two days. If we take the bank on Friday night we could have a nice little wad of money."

"They have two armed guards," said Harman. "Just how do you think you're gonna take the bank? I suppose all you have to do is ride in an' help yourselves."

"Somethin' like that," Hank agreed, sarcastically.

The sarcasm seemed lost on Luke Harman. "Mister!" he sighed. "Out here the banks have what they call a safe to keep their money in. I'd've thought that even the banks back east did that."

Hank laughed. "I'm not that simple! Sure, I know they'll have a safe. We should be able to blow it open easy enough with a couple of sticks of dynamite and I see you've got a couple of boxes of it over there." He nodded to the side of the room.

"An' just what the hell do you think the sheriff, the guards an' the rest of the folk in Appleby will be doin' while you is doin' all this?" sneered Harman.

"The five of us should be able to deal with them," assured Hank. "I'm pretty good with explosives so I'll be blowin' the safe while you lot keep the sheriff and anyone else at bay."

"What about the guards?" asked Irish.

"They'll be past carin' what's goin' on," Hank laughed.

"It all sounds too easy," said Irish.

"So have you any better ideas?" asked Hank. "Look at it this way. If you sit here and do nothin' the chances are that one day you'll still get caught or killed. I don't know what you are all wanted for, but me, I'm for swingin' on the end of a rope so I might as well at least try; sittin' on my arse isn't goin' to make the slightest difference."

"That goes for me too," said Slim. "I'm for the rope."

"Me too," said Bull. "I guess I've got nothin' to lose."

"At my age, the prospect of at least twenty years in the pen is not all that

73

inviting," said Irish. "OK, Mr Carter, you've convinced me."

Eli agreed that he was due for at least ten years and nodded his agreement. "We oughta know the layout of the bank," he suggested.

Hank looked at Harman. "Nobody knows that better'n you do. Give me a piece of paper and a pencil; let's have a look at the layout of the town and the inside of the bank."

"I don't see why the hell I should help you rob the bank I use!" snarled Harman. "That sounds kinda stupid to me."

Hank was suddenly on his feet and pushing the barrel of his Adams up Harman's nose. "It'd be even more stupid of you if you didn't!"

Harman tried to draw away from the gun but could not. "You'd kill me?"

"I killed me a judge and his two sons and that piece of trash you called Rosie, so the owner of a rundown tradin' post wouldn't present any problems.

Believe it, Harman, I'll kill you if I have to."

Luke Harman believed every word. "OK, OK, I'll go fetch the pencil an' paper . . . "

4

"HOW'S that horse of yours doin'?" Sheriff Weaver demanded as Brogan ambled slowly down the street towards him. "Five days it is now, she should be almost ready to ride out."

"Tomorrow, the doc reckons," replied Brogan. "Don't worry, I'll be on my way as soon as she's ready. Wouldn't want to outstay my welcome anywhere."

"You've already outstayed it!" grunted Weaver. "I've got to admit though, you've been a lot less trouble than I expected."

"Just what kinda trouble did you expect?"

Weaver smiled thinly. "Don't know for sure. I suppose I expected a spate of thievin' or somethin'."

"Strange as it may seem, Sheriff,"

Brogan grinned, "I ain't never done no thievin' in my life."

"That's the way most saddle bums live," said Weaver.

"Yeh," Brogan was forced to agree. "Some of 'em got a lot to answer for, they give decent folk like me a bad name."

"You ain't perfect," said Weaver. "Maybe you don't steal, leastways not where you can get caught, but you've gotta live. Where'd you get your money from?"

"Here an' there!" said Brogan, non-committally.

"Yeh!" Weaver sneered. "I still don't trust you an the sooner you're out of my territory the better pleased I'll be. I run a law-abidin' town an' I intend to keep it that way."

"Even with a bunch of hoodlums sittin' on your front doorstep?"

"They keep out!" said Weaver. "They know what'll happen if they so much as set one foot in my county."

"Maybe so," said Brogan. "Can't

help wonderin' what's happened to that feller I left in the desert though. He shoulda been out of there an' here by now."

"With a bit of luck he either died of thirst or he got himself killed at Harman's tradin' post."

"Harman!" said Brogan. "I can't see him bein' a wanted man. Don't he ever come into town?"

"Once a month usually," said Weaver. "Come to think of it he should be here now. There's some supplies waitin' for him at the railroad depot. It ain't like him to be late. I wonder where he is? Somethin' must've held him up."

Brogan did not like coincidences and it seemed rather more than pure chance that Luke Harman had not arrived in town and that Hank Carter must have reached the trading post. However, coincidence or not, it was of little concern to him, all he was concerned about was getting on his way, although as ever he had no idea where he was going.

★ ★ ★

Hank Carter looked down on Appleby, checking the description of the town given to him by Harman against what he could see through the spyglass. He was able to identify all the buildings, streets and approaches. The railroad depot stood amid a maze of cattle pens some three or four hundred yards beyond the neat, white painted church.

According to Harman the train passed through heading west three times a week on Monday, Wednesday and Friday and heading east on Tuesday, Thursday and Saturday. He had the impression that the west bound train had already passed through; the tiny station seemed to be stacked with boxes and parcels all gradually being taken away. If Harman had been correct, there should also have been quite a bit of extra money on the train, but that would now be safely installed in the bank.

The bank itself was a mud and

brick building standing on its own a few yards from the church. The rear of the bank looked out on to the cemetery whilst the front was almost directly opposite the sheriffs office. An armed guard stood on duty outside the bank and, if Harman was correct, there would be another inside.

"Looks easy enough!" declared Hank. "We can reach it by crossin' the cemetery, there's plenty of thick brush for cover the other side."

"Fine," said Bull, "but just how the hell are we gonna get in? Accordin' to Harman them walls is at least two feet thick, maybe even three."

"There's two doors," Hank pointed out. "The front door an' a small one at the back. That's the way we go in, the back door. Even if it does have a grille across, that'll be easy to deal with."

"I only hope you are right," said Irish. "I don't know why, but I have me this strange feelin' of impendin' doom. I've had it ever since you killed

80

Harman. Was that really necessary? He'd given us all the information we wanted."

"That was exactly why he had to be killed!" grated Hank. "He said himself that it was his day for goin' into Appleby. If we'd just let him go he would probably have blabbed everythin' to the sheriff."

"Maybe you're right!" sighed Irish. "That still doesn't calm this feelin' I have."

"When you're feelin' all that money you'll realize just how stupid you are!" Hank laughed.

"What time do we go in?" asked Slim.

"We wait until well after sunset," said Hank. "Give them all time to get in the saloon and have a few drinks. No man thinks too good after he's had a few whiskies."

"Now that's somethin' I wouldn't have thought of," said Irish. "See what I mean about me not thinkin' too good?"

"Me neither," agreed Bull. "Makes sense though."

"All right, make yourselves comfortable," said Hank. "We've got a few hours to wait."

★ ★ ★

A kind of understanding had developed between Sheriff Weaver and Brogan. Brogan was allowed to use the saloon during the day when hardly anyone else bothered and he kept away from it after about eight o'clock in the evening. The arrangement suited Brogan fine. He was not all that interested in drink except as a means of curing a thirst and he liked to turn in fairly early as well.

However, with little else to do, Brogan had developed the habit of going into the saloon at about six o'clock. He took his meals at Bess Pringle's and had managed to avoid her not too subtle advances. He was alone in the saloon when a dust covered figure hustled in demanding a beer.

"You'd better tell Luke Harman he forgot to lock up when he left this mornin'," the man said to the bartender. "I could've helped myself to everythin' he had. Even that trash that's been livin' there seem to have disappeared."

"I ain't seen Luke all day," said the bartender. "Hadn't given it much thought before, but I ain't seen him at all. He should've been here; there's some boxes for him at the railroad station, I saw 'em when I collected the whisky I'd ordered."

"All gone?" asked Brogan.

"That's what I said," replied the man. "All gone, bedrolls, horses, the lot."

"That don't make sense," said Brogan.

"Sense or not," said the man, gulping down his beer, "that's the way it is. Ain't no concern of mine though . . . Another beer!"

Brogan pondered the information for some time and, although it was of no concern of his whatsoever, there was something about it which bothered him.

Sheriff Weaver came into the saloon shortly after the man had finished his second beer and departed. The bartender seemed either to have forgotten what the man had said or did not think it any concern of his.

"Has this Luke Harman been in town?" Brogan asked the sheriff.

"Ain't seen him," said Weaver. "What you wanna know for?"

Brogan explained what had happened and that he considered it to be very strange.

"Those guys didn't have no need to suddenly skip out like that," he said, "an' this Luke Harman not comin' into town when he's supposed to makes it more suspicious."

"What's it to you?" asked Weaver. "All I can say is if that scum have decided to skip out then I for one ain't gonna lose too much sleep over it. As for Harman, he's his own man."

Brogan sighed. "You're right, Sheriff. Tomorrow I'll be on my way an' Appleby an' Luke Harman will be just names. All the same, somethin' don't sit right with me. A murderer crosses the desert an' he's got to end up at the tradin' post. The tradin' post has a bunch of hoodlums livin' there. Suddenly they all disappear an' the murderer still ain't showed up in Appleby. No, sir, somethin' don't sit right at all."

"You've lost me!" Weaver laughed. "Especially since it ain't no concern of yours at all."

"Yeh, you is right!" muttered Brogan. "All the same, I reckon there's gonna be some trouble; I just got me this feelin' an' my feelin's ain't very often wrong. I've spent my life heedin' my feelin's an' they've done pretty well by me so far."

Sheriff Weaver laughed. "I appreciate the warnin', McNally, but when the day comes that I have to listen to the likes of you, I'll resign or end up in a pine box."

"I warn't offerin' no advice," said Brogan, "Just tellin' you what I think. It don't bother me none what you choose to believe."

* * *

Hank Carter did not make his move until after ten o'clock, giving the citizens of Appleby plenty of time to become affected by the alcohol they were consuming. A little after ten o'clock he led his men out of the hills and down towards the town, carefully skirting it and coming in behind the cemetery.

Each man had been well briefed in what his exact role was to be and, leaving their horses in the dense brush behind the cemetery, each quite easily found his way to his allotted position. Hank Carter headed for the rear door of the bank and waited behind a solitary bush for a while, anticipating that the guard may well be making regular checks of the premises. He could hardly believe his luck as a guard opened the back door, scratched himself and then locked the door behind him with a key attached to a long chain around his waist, before heading slowly for the bush where Hank was hiding. He seemed intent on relieving himself against the bush. That was when Hank moved . . .

★ ★ ★

"I thought I told you the saloon was out of bounds to you at this time of night!" grated Sheriff Weaver when he saw Brogan enter.

"I ain't arguin'," said Brogan. "Right now I reckon you got company, company what seems intent on robbin' your bank."

Both men were standing by the door and the Sheriff steered Brogan outside and looked across the street at the bank, still showing the light which was always lit at night, and the figure of a guard sitting at a desk.

"Everythin' looks OK to me," the sheriff laughed. "So where are these men then?"

"They came across the graveyard," said Brogan. "I'd say five or six of 'em."

Once again Weaver laughed, this time slapping Brogan across the shoulder. "Now I know you're loco, McNally. I reckon you've been at the whiskey an' now you're seein' ghosts. Well I don't believe in ghosts an' as far as I'm concerned everythin' looks perfectly normal. Good night, McNally, I'll be glad when you can leave, which should be tomorrow with any luck!"

"Don't say I didn't warn you," said Brogan.

"Don't worry, I won't!" Weaver laughed loudly, slapped Brogan across the shoulder again and returned to the saloon.

Brogan thought for a moment before shrugging his shoulders and disappearing into the shadows.

* * *

Brogan knew he was not mistaken. In matters such as this he knew he was never mistaken. He was quite proud of the fact that he could detect alien movement anywhere and this time he had definitely detected the movement of at least five men from the thick brush and across the graveyard. He had also heard the click of a key turning and the subsequent dying gasp.

He had tried to warn Sheriff Weaver, but knew that nothing else he could say would convince the man. He seriously thought of returning to his bed in the stable and await the outcome; it was, as the sheriff had pointed out, no business or concern of his. However, Brogan McNally was not like that, in fact if something bothered him he had to worry it until he had discovered what it was or had put it to rights. Perhaps those who said he was too nosy for his own good were nearer the truth. Whatever the reason, Brogan was bound to find out more.

Even skirting well clear of the bank, Brogan was able to pinpoint three men in the shadows. However, he was not interested in tackling any of them, he had another idea . . .

★ ★ ★

The guard died easily and, Hank thought, very quietly. He quickly removed the keys from the guard's waist and then dragged the body under the bush. Stopping to listen for a very short time that there were no problems, he slowly made his way to the back door of the bank.

There were five keys on the ring and he found the key he wanted at the second attempt. On opening the door, he cursed under his breath when he found that there was an inner door in the form of a large grille.

The room beyond was in darkness, but there was a light shining from under a door at the far end. He had to assume that the other guard was in there. Working as quietly as possible, he managed to find the correct key and slowly opened the grille. To his horror it opened with a loud creak.

"That you, Andy?" The call came from the office.

"Uhuh!" responded Hank, leaving both the grille door and the rear door open for a quick escape. He slowly felt his way in the dark room towards the office.

He knew from what Luke Harman had told him, that it was a company rule that at least one of the guards must always be in full view of the sheriffs office opposite. His problem was how to try and open the safe whilst still giving the impression that all was well. The rules were quite specific. If there was no guard in the office then the sheriff had to act.

He opened the door slightly, enough for him to be able to see inside without being seen himself. A quick glance across the street at the sheriffs office showed him that all was perfectly clear.

"One sound out of you and you're dead!" Hank rasped.

The guard involuntarily rose to his feet but he was too late. He was so intent on the gun in Hank's hand that he failed to see the knife . . .

Working very quickly, Hank arranged the body in the chair to give the impression that all was well. He had not acted a moment too soon . . .

Despite laughing at Brogan's claim of men surrounding the bank, Sheriff Weaver did feel slightly uneasy and to reassure himself that all was well, he left the saloon and wandered back to his office. The scene in the bank appeared perfectly normal and the figure inside even waved as he tapped on the window. He shook his head and returned to the saloon, convinced that he had been right; Brogan McNally had been in the sun too long.

Hank Carter breathed more easily. He was quite confident of being able to deal with the sheriff and anyone else in town, but he did not want any fighting until he was ready. He had seen the sheriff walk across the street and willed his men not to act and had flattened himself against the side of the desk and, when the sheriff had tapped the window, he had raised the dead man's hand in acknowledgement and hoped that it had convinced the sheriff.

Before killing the judge, Hank Carter had worked for some two years in a bank, so he had a pretty good idea of the weaknesses of safes. In fact he had often fantasized about robbing a bank.

He smiled wryly when he lit a lamp and went into the main body of the bank. The safe was quite an old one of a model out of date even when he worked in the bank and he knew where the weak spots were.

"One stick of dynamite, plenty of paddin' and it should go easy enough. Thank God it isn't a more up-to-date safe. Now, somethin' to pad round it?"

The padding came in the form of a high backed leather chair and an upended desk, the whole finally covered with a large rug. The single stick of dynamite had been firmly wedged in position and, after double checking, Hank lit the fuse and rapidly retreated into another small room.

The explosion shattered the chair, sent large splinters of wood from the desk flying across the room and the blast shattered every window and the safe door swung open. Hank whooped with joy and scrambled into the safe, finding a sack inside already half full of money. He greedily stuffed as much of the other cash as he could into the sack just as the sound of gunfire came from outside.

* * *

For a few seconds all sound in the saloon ceased as everyone looked at each other in surprise. They were unsure what to make of the sudden explosion; even Sheriff Weaver had momentary doubts as to what it could be, but he was suddenly dashing from the saloon, commanding others to join him.

Appleby was a peaceful town: in fact it had been peaceful for so long that nobody ever carried a gun, there had never been any need. The result was that Sheriff Weaver was the only person who was armed and it was quite plain that his own gun against the four or five ranged against him was useless. Someone else did manage to produce a gun from somewhere but, trying to fire at unseen and unknown targets as they were, there was never any contest.

★ ★ ★

Hank crashed through the rear door and called out to his men to "Get the hell out of it" and he ran across the cemetery, conscious that the others were close behind. He smiled in triumph as he came to the brush where the horses were and listened.

The town seemed to be in uproar, but there did not appear to be anyone following. The others almost crashed into him as they scrambled over the small, low wall surrounding the cemetery.

"How much?" panted Bull.

"How the hell do I know!" rasped Hank. "We'll count it later. Right now let's get the hell out of here while we can."

They ran through the brush to where they had left their horses and stood around panting.

"Where the hell are they?" demanded Slim. "They was here, mine was tied to that bush over there!"

"It can't be the place!" gasped Hank. "Search for 'em!"

A rapid search followed to growing signs of others heading in their direction, but the horses were not to be found. Suddenly a voice called out.

"They ain't there! I moved 'em!"

"Who the hell is that?" demanded Hank.

"It don't matter none," came the reply. "You've had it, best give yourselves up."

"I recognize that voice!" declared Hank. "McNally! McNally, you no-good bastard! I'm goin' to kill you for this."

"Don't think so," called Brogan. "Nice try, Carter, full marks for tryin', but this is as far as you go."

"We'll see!" yelled Hank, firing in the general direction of the voice. "I ain't finished yet!"

By now the townsfolk had managed to organize themselves and were rapidly closing in. A few shots fell harmlessly close by, but the five began shooting in all directions.

Sheriff Weaver despatched men to surround the brush and for some time a battle raged, nobody able to see who or what they were firing at. Slowly the ring of townsfolk closed in and it became obvious to the men in the brush that they stood little chance, especially since they were rapidly running out of ammunition.

"OK, OK!" yelled Bull. "Don't shoot, we're comin' out!"

"Drop your guns an' come out with your hands raised!" came the order from Sheriff Weaver. "Nice an' slow; one false move an' you're all dead men!"

"We hear you!" called Bull, dropping his gun.

Weaver ordered all shooting to stop and wait until the men showed themselves. Very slowly three men came from the brush, their arms raised and they were quickly taken.

"Three of you?" demanded Weaver. "There's gotta be more, where are they?"

"Still in there as far as we know," grated Eli Smith. "Two more, an' that's all."

"Come on out!" commanded Weaver again. "You've got one minute, after that we're comin' in an' this time you won't have the chance to give yourselves up!"

Very few people heard it, and those who did gave it little thought, but the sound of horses riding away was heard. One who did hear it and did realize what had happened was Brogan McNally.

"They got away!" he called to Sheriff Weaver. "Must've took a couple of horses from the street."

"McNally! Where are you?" called Weaver.

"Just collectin' somethin'," called Brogan, "be with you in a minute. Just tell them guns of yours not to shoot, I'm on your side remember."

Weaver gave the order not to shoot and after a couple of minutes Brogan appeared at his side, carrying a sack.

"What you got there?" demanded the sheriff.

"Somethin' I reckon the bank will be mighty pleased to see," replied Brogan. "Two of 'em may have got away, but they didn't take the cash with 'em."

Sheriff Weaver took charge of the sack and ordered some men to search the brush just in case the other two were still hiding. The three who had given themselves up were bundled back to the small jail alongside the sheriffs office.

Sheriff Weaver locked the sack in his office before going to see who they had captured. Brogan was already there and he was not too surprised to find that Hank Carter was not one of the three.

"Well now," said Weaver as he joined the crowd in front of the jail. "Who have we here?" A lamp had been lit and he surveyed his prisoners. "Bull Plain, Eli Smith an' Slim Jones, not a bad haul for one night. Who were the ones who got away?"

"A stupid bastard called Hank Carter an' Paddy McMahon!" muttered Bull.

"Seems it was you who are the stupid bastards!" laughed Weaver.

"Yeh, guess so!" grumbled Eli. "We

shouldn't've listened to that slick talkin' city feller."

Bull looked hard at Brogan and snarled, "It was you, wasn't it, you stinkin' bastard? It was you what took our horses!"

"Couldn't think of any other way to stop you," Brogan grinned.

Weaver touched Brogan's arm and nodded towards his office. "I guess I've got an apology to make, but maybe you'd better explain."

Brogan nodded and followed the sheriff into his office where he explained about the horses. Knowing that he would not be believed, he had gone to the brush and simply led the horses away. Sheriff Weaver once again apologized, which rather went against the grain, but he was big enough to accept that he had been wrong.

The bodies of the two guards were recovered, the three men in jail told that it was likely that they would be charged with murder, to which they protested loudly claiming, correctly, that it had been the work of Hank Carter. The sheriff was inclined to believe them, but still held the threat of a murder charge over their heads.

5

THE following morning, the full extent of the damage to the bank was plain to see. Sheriff Weaver had personally mounted guard over the wreckage, just in case some of the less honest citizens of Appleby had any thoughts about helping themselves to anything, although, with the assistance of the bank staff, all the money had been removed and placed in the sheriffs office.

The sack recovered by Brogan had contained $26,400 and, after balancing the books, all monies that should have been in the bank were accounted for.

Although Brogan had thought about it, it was the president of the bank who raised the subject of a reward.

"Under the circumstances," said the president, "I think it only fair that we should show our gratitude to

Mr McNally in some way." Sheriff Weaver and the Mayor of Appleby were, somewhat reluctantly, forced to agree. "Quite obviously there is nothing we can offer Mr McNally which would be of any use to him other than cash. I therefore propose that the bank reward his foresight and ingenuity by offering him the sum of . . . " — he hesitated slightly, — "one hundred dollars . . . "

"Much appreciated," Brogan interrupted, "but the usual is ten per cent an' on twenty-six thousand that comes to twenty-six hundred dollars . . . "

"Now hold on there . . . " complained the mayor, "I think one hundred is more than fair, especially for a man like you."

"A man like me?" Brogan laughed. "Let me remind all of you that if it hadn't been for a man like me this town an' bank would've been twenty-six thousand dollars poorer. It wouldn't've mattered to me none if they had've got clear away. I didn't have to risk my life, 'specially since all any of you wanted to do was get me out of town as soon as possible. The reward out on them three alone must come to about six hundred dollars. I tell you what, you keep your hundred dollars, I'll just take the reward money."

"You're not entitled to any reward!" said Sheriff Weaver. "It wasn't you who caught them."

"That's somethin' of a debatable point," said Brogan. "Look, I ain't a feller what wants to cause any trouble an' all I need is enough money to see me through. I may not need much, but one hundred dollars is almost insultin' under the circumstances."

"Yes, well," mumbled the president of the bank. "I suppose we could consider a little more . . . I shall have to consult with the sheriff and the mayor . . . "

"An' I've got to consult with Doc Vernon about my horse," said Brogan. "Just let me know what you decide."

When Brogan had gone, it was the

mayor who felt that Brogan need not be offered any reward at all, claiming that there was nothing he could do about it if they did not.

"On a matter of principle," said the president, "I cannot agree. What is the legal position regarding the reward money, Sheriff?"

"I reckon he's entitled to it," said Weaver. "In any event the town can claim it, but he's got a good case for first choice."

"Then I believe we must offer it to Mr McNally," the president insisted. "He is right, he could quite legally claim his percentage from the bank."

"All I want is to see him ride out of here," said Weaver. "Since last night he's come to be somethin' of a hero an' I don't reckon it's healthy havin' a man like him hangin' about influencin' our youngsters or our women. He's dirty an' he smells, but I overheard two women just before I came in sayin' as how they thought he was a very attractive man."

"You're right!" said the president. "I suggest we offer him five hundred on condition that he rides out today. If he insists on more he'll have to wait around while it gets sorted out."

"I still think we could get away with giving him nothing!" said the mayor. "But I agree we've got to get rid of him as soon as possible. Very well, five hundred dollars and not one cent more."

★ ★ ★

Doc Vernon gave Brogan's horse the all clear and Brogan was more than pleased to accept the five hundred dollars. In actual fact he would have taken the one hundred, had they insisted. Five hundred was far more than he had had in his pocket for a long time and would last him quite a considerable time, making it easier to avoid people and towns, using out-of-the-way trading posts.

He left Appleby with the minimum of

fuss and headed west, the direction he had been going, more or less following the railroad, although he eventually decided to head up into the mountains, where he felt more at home.

He had purchased plenty of supplies, so as yet there was no need to hunt and up in the mountains there was plenty of grass for his horse and water for both of them.

The thought as to what had happened to Hank Carter and the one called Paddy MacMahon briefly crossed his mind, but the thought did not linger, such thoughts never did. He did not even wonder what would happen if he ever met up with them.

However, on the second day out from Appleby, he did have cause to think about them again.

The valley he was riding along was very narrow and very deep, the sides rising upwards of a thousand feet and even more. There was no way he could avoid the homestead which stood on a piece of high ground above the river and, as far as he was concerned, there was no reason why he should avoid it. However, it seemed that the occupants of the homestead had other ideas.

The bullet passed by harmlessly enough and he realized that it was probably intended as a warning, but he still objected to being shot at when there was no apparent reason. One thing he did know however, was that country folk never shot at anyone or anything unless there was a reason so, although he did not know what it was, he accepted that there was probably a valid reason in the mind of whoever fired the gun.

"Now hold on!" Brogan called out, dropping off his horse and hiding behind a large rock. "You ain't got no cause to do that, I ain't done nothin'!"

"That's what them other two said!" came a female voice in reply. "That didn't stop them shootin' my man though."

"What they do that for?" Brogan called.

"They wanted me, that's why!" she replied. "My George wouldn't let 'em take me, so they shot him an' then took me!"

"Hell ma'am," said Brogan, sincerely, "sorry to hear that. I sure can understand how you feel, but I ain't like that. If you like I'll just ride on by an' leave you to bury your man . . . "

"He ain't dead!" she said. "Leastways not yet." She was beginning to sound a little desperate. "Are you alone?"

"Yes, ma'am," assured Brogan.

"Do you know anythin' about bullet wounds?"

"I seen a few in my time," said Brogan.

"Have you ever dug a bullet out of a man?" she persisted.

"No ma'am, I can honestly say I never have," he replied. "I've put a few in a few men, but never had cause to take none out. There's always a first time though, I guess. If you like I'll see what I can do. I've had to treat enough cuts an' things before now, so I guess takin' a bullet out is somethin' similar an' I have seen a doctor do it a couple of times."

"You can come up to the house!" the woman called. "Don't try anythin' though, I've got you covered. I may not be much use as a nurse, but I am one helluva good shot."

"Why didn't you kill me then?" asked Brogan.

"Maybe I should have!" she said. "Maybe I will."

"Ain't no need for that ma'am," said Brogan, trying to look friendly. "I promise you I don't intend no harm."

"I'll keep the gun on you till I'm sure!" insisted the woman.

She was very young; Brogan guessed she was about seventeen or eighteen, and very pretty. He wondered just why such a pretty young woman should choose to live out here. He noted that she did handle the rifle with a great deal of confidence and knowledge and decided that she did indeed know exactly how to handle it.

She nodded inside the house and Brogan went in. The single room was very clean and furnished with all the trappings of a woman only recently married and still in full flush of enjoying keeping house for her man. The man himself was lying on the bed covered by a blanket, which showed a deep red stain at about chest level.

Brogan pulled back the blanket and revealed the young, slim body of a man not much older than the woman. There was very little colour in him and even Brogan could tell that he had lost a lot of blood.

He gently removed the bandage from around the boy's chest, at least Brogan considered him little more than a boy, to show a messy, gaping wound. Brogan had seen worse, but only on dead men.

"Must've been mighty close to put a hole that size in him," he said. "Don't know much about these things, but I'd say he was very lucky, it must've missed his heart, else he'd be dead by now."

"Can you get the bullet out?" she urged, still keeping a tight hold on the rifle.

"Don't look to me like there's any need," replied Brogan. "Have you had a good look?" She shook her head. "I reckon it must've passed right through."

He gently turned the boy on to his side and stripped back the blood soaked shirt. There was another hole in his back and Brogan nodded, somewhat satisfied that he had been proved right.

"You . . . you must think I'm . . . " started the girl.

"I don't think nothin', ma'am," said Brogan, letting the boy return to lie on his back. "The wound looks clean enough, but I reckon it oughta be washed or somethin', leastways get rid of all that dried blood." He looked up at the girl and smiled slightly. "Put that damned rifle down: I ain't gonna hurt you. You can make yourself useful an' get some hot water, bandages or clean rags, an' help me clean him up."

She looked at Brogan for a few seconds, unsure whether to believe him or not, finally deciding that she did. "There's hot water on the fire," she said. "I ain't got no bandages, all I got is a clean sheet."

"That'll do fine," said Rogan. "Rip it up into long strips about six inches wide."

The girl took a sheet out of cupboard and proceeded to cut it up as instructed while Brogan began the task of cleaning the boy up.

"Do you think he'll live?" she asked, choking back a sob.

"I ain't no doctor," said Brogan. "When did this happen?"

"Yesterday," she replied. "Yesterday mornin'. They rode in, two of 'em, askin' for food an' then they said they wanted me. That's when George got shot, 'cos he tried to stop 'em." She choked back another tear. "Damned

114

fool! He should've let 'em; at least they probably wouldn't've shot him. It was that horrible little Irishman who shot him."

Brogan's interest was suddenly aroused. "Irishman? You sure about that ma'am?"

"He was an Irishman all right," she assured. "I've got some Irish friends, so I know the accent. An' don't keep callin' me 'ma'am', the name's Annie."

"Well if them two is who I think they is," said Brogan. "I reckon they'd've been just as likely to kill your man even if he'd not tried to stop 'em. Did you hear the name of the other man?"

"Carter!" she replied. "Yes, Carter. I remember the Irishman called him Mr Carter. I thought it was strange, the Irishman was a lot older than the other one, he was bout my George's age, but he called him Mr Carter at least three times."

Brogan shook his head sadly. "Hell, I thought I'd seen an' heard the last of them two! They is just the kind of trouble I could do without. Mind, it's p'raps as well I happened along. I reckon if your man had been left to you, you'd've just stood by an' waited for him to die."

She bit her knuckle and moaned. "I know! I know! I . . . I just didn't know what to do. Do you think he'll be all right?"

"He's survived this long, despite you," said Brogan rather unkindly. "I reckon he's got a good chance of pullin' through."

She knelt alongside her man and took his limp hand. "Please, George, don't die on me, please!"

"You been married long?" asked Brogan, strapping the wound.

"Two weeks!" she said, gazing at him with large, watery eyes.

"Then I guess you've still got a lot to learn," said Brogan, smiling kindly. "Didn't your mother ever teach you what to do about things like this? Most women I ever come across seemed to know better'n the doctor sometimes."

"No," admitted Annie. "I'm not a country girl, I'm a city girl. I guess there was never any need to teach me, there was always a doctor handy."

"City girl?" said Brogan. "What the hell you doin' out here then? This place couldn't be anythin' further from a city."

She smiled weakly. "It was George. He's country born an' bred. He was workin' for my pa, but he couldn't really take to city life. By that time we'd decided to get married. Ma an' Pa did try to warn me about what it would be like, but I guess I was too much in love to listen — I still am."

"Where's the nearest doctor?" asked Brogan.

"I suppose there must be one in Kenton."

"How far's that?"

"I don't know for sure, I think it's about a day's ride away."

"You don't know?"

"I haven't been there yet," she

confessed, "but George told me about it. I know they've got a church and a general store, but not much else, not much else I know about it I mean."

"Well I reckon he ought to see a doctor," said Brogan. "Do you reckon you can get him to this place, what did you call it? Kenton."

"We've got a buckboard and a horse," she said. "I suppose I could get him there. I've no idea what the road is like though."

Brogan sighed and shook his head. "I guess I ain't got no option but to go with you. Don't want to, but I ain't so sure that you'd be able to get through on your own."

"I can manage!" she pouted.

"Like you managed to stop your man bleedin' almost to death?" Brogan could not help being a little sarcastic.

"That was different!" she answered sharply. "I've been brought up to handle a gun and a wagon."

"Thought you was city bred?" said Brogan.

"So I am!" she replied, proudly straightening her back and raising her head somewhat defiantly. "My father always insisted on all his children, girls as well as boys, an' there was four of each, being able to handle a gun and we do have horses and buggies an' things in cities as well you know."

"It's one thing drivin' in a city an' quite another drivin' somewhere like up here," Brogan pointed out.

"Don't worry about me Mr . . . er . . . "

"Just call me Brogan," he replied. "I didn't mean no offence. I'm quite sure you probably can manage to drive the buckboard, providin' the road's good, but if I know this type of country you is just liable to find the trail blocked by a rock fall or a tree or somethin'."

"I'll manage!" she insisted.

"Look ma'am . . . " — he could not bring himself to call her by her name — "it seems I gotta go that way anyhow, so I might as well go with you. I can always leave you an' go my own way. Probably will; I ain't got no need to go into no town, not yet awhile that is."

She thought about it for a moment. "I guess so," she agreed. "Sorry if I seemed a bit . . . well, you know . . . I've just been raped by two men an' I'm not too sure about any man after a thing like that."

"Ma'am," Brogan smiled, "I guess I'm old enough to be your grandfather, just about . . . "

"Since when did that make any difference?" she laughed.

"I guess it don't really," he admitted. "You ain't got no need to worry though, I ain't interested."

"I ought to feel insulted!" she laughed. "Thanks anyhow, I somehow kinda believe you don't intend no harm."

"I'll go fix up the buckboard," said Brogan. "You get yourself an' him some things together, I reckon you is gonna need 'em, he'll probably have to rest up awhile."

"He has a brother just outside

Kenton," said Annie. "I haven't met him or his wife yet, but I'm sure they'll help."

"I'm sure they will," Brogan nodded. "Take somethin' to wrap round yourself an' him, somethin' good an' warm, just in case it takes longer'n a day. Maybe you'd better take some food as well."

"An' a gun!" she said, picking up her rifle. "I hope I don't need it, but they're still out there!"

"I know that, ma'am," he said. "I've been thinkin' about that too. That's one more reason I ought to go with you."

"You seem to know these men," said Annie. "Are you some sort of lawman or somethin', or one of them bounty hunters I've heard about?"

"Lawman!" he laughed. "I did have a shot at it once; I ain't quite sure now how I let myself be talked into it. No, ma'am . . . "

"Annie!" she insisted.

"Annie," he nodded. "No, I ain't no lawman nor a bounty hunter, not regular that is, although I have collected bounty now an' then, mostly when I was short of money an' there just happened to be someone around with a price on their head."

"What are you then?"

"Saddle tramp!" he said, rather proudly. "Thought you would've noticed the smell, leastways folk reckon I smell on account I don't believe in bathin' an' soap an' hot water."

Annie wrinkled her nose slightly. "I had noticed that you had a certain . . . er . . . aroma."

"You mean I stink!" he laughed. "Don't matter none to me what folk think, it sure ain't gonna make me feel guilty an' start usin' soap."

"Yeh, you stink!" she laughed. Brogan laughed too, it helped relieve the tension and made her relax a little. "How do you know these men then?"

"I ain't never met the Irishman," he admitted. "I met the one called Carter somethin' over a week ago, out in the desert. He'd lost his horse an' I fed him some rattlesnake I'd caught . . . "

"I've heard about eating snake," she said, shuddering slightly.

"Sure tastes good when you is starvin'!" he grinned. "Anyhow, I fed this Carter an' then let him walk out the desert on his own. I hear he's got a good reward out on him, two thousand dollars alive was the last I heard. Don't know about the Irishman, probably only a couple of hundred."

"Two thousand!" exclaimed Annie. "We sure could do with that kind of money! What did he do to be worth that much?"

"Murdered a judge!" replied Brogan. "Now, if you don't mind, we'll do less jawin' now an' more doin', we won't get started before sundown else."

"I don't expect we shall reach Kenton before nightfall," she said. "George said it was a good day's ride on a horse, not on one pullin' a wagon."

"Then the sooner we start off the better!" said Brogan.

He soon found the horse and

buckboard and led them round to the front of the house. The buckboard was literally that, a board. Apart from the driver's seat, it consisted of a wide board between two sets of wheels.

He carefully carried the unconscious George out of the cabin and placed him on the board, wrapped him in a blanket and decided that he would have to strap him to the board.

"If he falls off it could do more damage!" explained Brogan. "You can ride an' drive, I'll be ridin' my horse."

"That suits me," said Annie, tying a basket of food to the seat alongside her and stowing the rifle into the holder on the side of the seat. "I've brought some extra ammunition as well."

Brogan laughed. "For a girl what hadn't got the faintest idea what to do to stop her husband bleedin' to death, you sure seem well organized."

"That was different," she defended. "I was in a state of shock: I couldn't think straight."

"Well you just start thinkin' about

steerin' that wagon proper," he warned. "One thing we can do without is a busted axle or wheel, we'll never get to this Kenton else."

"You just concentrate on doin' whatever it is you do an' leave me to look after the wagon!" she scolded.

Brogan watched as she started off and, after less than half a mile over pretty rough ground, he decided that she was quite a capable young lady and that her first reactions must have been due to the shock of being raped and the shooting of her husband.

6

IT very quickly became obvious to Brogan that there was absolutely no chance of making it to Kenton either that day or the next, unless the condition of the track improved greatly. On his own, it was quite likely that the town was well within less than a day, but the rocky, pitted track had not been made with a wagon in mind.

"How the hell did you get out here?" he asked Annie during one of the all too frequent occasions when he was forced to clear boulders out of the way.

"We came out on horseback," she replied with a knowing grin. "I think the buckboard had been made out on the farm. We had two horses then. I don't know what happened to the other one, but we found her dead a couple of mornin's after we got here."

Brogan looked up at the almost sheer sides of the narrow valley they were travelling along and shook his head. The lower slopes were thickly wooded but the higher slopes, rising to about a thousand feet, were almost sheer rock.

"Seems one hell of a place to choose to live," he said. "What kinda farmin' can you do here?"

"We thought about sheep," she replied. "George found some gold, not a lot I think, but he reckons there's enough to live on even if we don't take up sheep. We've got a couple of cows an' three goats an' there's plenty of game to hunt an' fish in the rivers. All in all, there's no need for us to starve."

"That's for sure," agreed Brogan. "Even a man like me'd be hard put to go hungry out here, but that ain't everythin', leastways I don't reckon it'd be enough for the likes of you. I don't know 'bout these things, certainly not from experience since I ain't never been wed, but even a newly married couple is gonna find life pretty borin' stuck out here on your own."

Annie smiled and sighed a little. "It's beautiful, it really is, but I've got to confess that I've never known so much rain in my life. I do miss socializin', I can't say as I don't, but I chose the man an' his way of life, so I guess I've got to make the best of it."

"You say you've never been to Kenton?" asked Brogan.

"No, never had cause, everythin' was at the farm."

"What about this brother?"

"Steve," she said. "I think he's George's elder brother. I've never met him either. We did send a wire to Kenton tellin' him we were married, but I don't know a thing about them, 'ceptin' he's a hunter or somethin'."

"Good huntin' country too, I reckon," said Brogan.

An hour later the trail was joined by another from a valley very similar to the one they had been travelling along and, at the fork, there was a battered old signpost, long since fallen over, but the single arm indicated that Kenton was another thirty miles. Now Brogan knew for certain that it was going to be another two days.

It was about an hour to sundown, but the high sides of the valley and the mountain peaks towering above had hidden the sun earlier on in the afternoon. He decided that now was as good a time as any to rest up for the night.

He told Annie to pull the buckboard up on to a piece of higher, flatter ground well out of reach of any flash flooding of the river and under the shelter of the trees. He unhitched the horse from the buckboard and unsaddled his own before collecting wood for a fire.

He was forced to smile at the things Annie produced from the basket she had brought with her. There was a cake, some cookies, half a loaf of fresh bread and some thinly sliced meat.

"Sure is obvious you ain't no country

girl," he said, laughing kindly. "What you got there's more in keepin' with a Sunday School picnic."

"You eat your snake if you want to!" she pouted. "I like to know what I'm eating. Besides, it's not as if we're crossing a desert or going for a week, is it?"

"No offence!" he laughed. "I guess it'll make a change to eat good food."

"I've put up enough for two!" she said.

"Don't reckon so, ma'am," he smiled. "See that sign back there, that says Kenton is another two days. I reckon tomorrow night you might just be tryin' snake."

"Never!" she scorned defiantly. "I'd rather starve."

"We'll see!" he laughed.

He had to admit that the cake and cookies tasted good, it had been a long time since he had eaten such things. Even Bess Pringle in Appleby had not provided cake or cookies. The meat too was well cooked and tasty, obviously deer meat, but the amount she had brought was not, in his opinion, even enough for one hungry man, let alone two people for two days or more. He decided that Annie still had a lot to learn, but she would learn.

After they had eaten, they sat by the fire chatting about nothing in particular when he suddenly waved his hand to silence her.

"You reckon it was yesterday them two came through?" he whispered.

"Yes!" she replied, hoarsely and looking nervously around. "What is it?"

"Could be nothin'," he replied, trying to sound reassuring. "Most likely ain't nothin', but I thought I heard somethin'."

Annie laughed lightly. "Out here! There's nothin' else but noise! Listen to it, you can hardly hear yourself for the birds and I expect if you did hear anythin' it was probably some deer."

"I expect you're right!" he said, with a grin.

If there was one thing Brogan could sense, it was the presence of something that did not belong. He had already established at least two deer close by but the one thing that gave him the vital clue was a sudden flight of birds. He had not seen them but he had heard them plainly enough. He knew very well that birds did not take fright from things like deer, only something that should not be there, just as he and Annie had put birds to flight all along the trail.

He was distinctly uneasy, although he tried not to show it for her sake, especially as she was now tending her injured husband. He stood up, stretched and made an excuse about having to obey the call of nature, which she seemed to accept, and he disappeared among the trees in the direction of the disturbance.

There was nothing to be seen or heard, but he knew that something was amiss, every fibre in his body was screaming at him and such feelings were not often, if ever, wrong.

"There's two things you can do," he said to himself. "Either hide up here somewheres or go up above the tree line an' see what you can."

"Ain't a lot of use waitin' here," he replied. "Trees are so thick they could pass real close an' not be seen."

"You must be gettin' old!" he scolded himself. "I thought you could hear a fly land on a piece of shit from a hundred yards away?"

"We sure ain't gettin' no younger!" he replied. "I say we go up above the tree line."

"What about her?"

"I reckon she'll be all right," he said. "I'll tell her to keep her gun handy though."

He returned to Annie and told her that he thought someone was prowling around and that he was going to investigate. She picked up her rifle, checked it and did not attempt to talk him out of what he was doing.

Brogan listened for a while and

eventually made his way through the trees until he was forced to climb. The tree line was reached very quickly and he found himself on a narrow ledge overlooking the river. Although it was now dark, there was sufficient light from the almost full moon to give him a good picture of what was below. Owls and bats could be seen as ghostly shadows and even a solitary deer slaking its thirst in the clear, moonlit river had a slightly unreal appearance.

Unreal or not, the deer suddenly vanished into the safety of the surrounding trees. Brogan stared hard and for a few moments nothing happened. Gradually he became aware of movement further along the trail which seemed to be heading in the direction of Annie and the buckboard.

Two riders appeared, moving very slowly and in the moonlight it was impossible to make out who they were, although the general descriptions certainly matched those of Hank Carter and the Irishman. They were still about two hundred yards from Annie and Brogan decided that he had seen enough and began to make his way back.

★ ★ ★

It was daylight when Brogan came to. He blinked groggily at the coarse bark of a pine tree which, it appeared, had somehow come into contact with his head. He tried moving but winced in pain as his right leg did not seem to want to move. He managed to look in the general direction of his feet and after a few seconds of bringing things into focus, he could just make out that his foot was wedged between two saplings.

Saplings they may have been, but he had the utmost difficulty in detaching foot from wedge. Eventually he managed it and struggled to his feet checking himself over as he did so.

Apart from a couple of cuts on his face and forehead a bit of bruising and general stiffness, there did not appear to be anything else wrong. He glanced up at the sky and, even through the thick overhead canopy, he realized that it must be at least three hours since sunrise.

He looked ruefully up the sheer wall of rock behind him and noted the obvious path of his unintended descent. He estimated that he must have fallen a good fifty feet and was even more surprised that he had not suffered any broken bones at the very least.

He did think about running back to where Annie had been left, but years of experience told him that it would serve no purpose. If she had waited for him she would still be there, but it was most unlikely that she was there. Even if the two visitors the previous night had been friendly, she surely must have told them about him and they would more than likely have heard his fall.

"She's either gone or they took her

or they killed her!" he muttered to himself, trying hard not to slip on the fine surface of pine needles.

"I'll lay odds we find her body!" he replied.

"You're on!" he muttered.

The scene was very much as he had left it the previous evening: the buckboard was still there, George was still on it, Annie's basket was on the seat and her horse was contentedly chomping at the grass. The one difference was that his old horse was nowhere to be seen.

He did call her, but he did not really expect any answer. It was obvious to him that she had been taken along with Annie. There were distinct signs of a struggle and he made out the imprints of two sets of male shoes and one set of smaller ones he assumed to be those of Annie.

George seemed to be alive and it did not appear that anyone had done anything to him, quite content to leave him for dead. Brogan looked up at a rock and smiled a solitary buzzard who was also hoping that George had been left for dead.

"Sorry, fella! Not this time!" called Brogan. The bird seemed to understand and slowly spread its wings and took off in majestic flight.

"So what the hell you gonna do with him?" Brogan asked himself.

"I suppose we ain't got much choice," he replied. "Can't leave him here. Only thing we can do is get him to this Kenton place."

"An' what about her?" he asked.

"Ain't that much we can do about her right now," he replied. "Can't go chasin' about these damned mountains haulin' a half-dead man after us. 'Sides, if we is to go after her, we'll need a better nag than this one, she's even worse'n ours."

"Get him to Kenton, tell the sheriff all about it an' then get the hell out of it!" he advised himself.

"Can't leave her with them!" he insisted.

"Annie'll just have to look after herself!"

"I didn't mean Annie, I meant our horse! We've been together too long to be split up now."

"I guess you just talked us into it!" he said to himself.

Having talked himself into the only action he could have taken, Brogan hitched the horse up to the buckboard and began what he knew would be a long, slow, bumpy journey to Kenton. Luckily he had recovered his rifle from where he had landed and it appeared undamaged.

The trail showed little sign of improving and he had to make frequent stops to move rocks or fallen trees. Fortunately for him none of the trees were so big that they could not be moved, although it was touch and go with one or two of the larger boulders. Three times he was forced to use the rope which secured George to the buckboard, tie it round a rock and get the horse to do the heavy work.

The rope was beginning to wear a bit thin and he had serious doubts as to its ability to pull another boulder out of the way.

After about four hours he came across another trail joining from the right and again a drunken signpost which indicated that Kenton was still twenty miles away.

However, it was not the distance to Kenton which dismayed him, but a note pinned to the signpost. He had the feeling even before he unfolded it and read it that it was intended for him.

I am watching you, McNally — I can see you but you can't see me. I've got the girl — I don't know what she is to you but if you want her you'll have to come and get her. It's you I want, not her, although she is very good. Hank Carter.

Brogan found that he was not too surprised and he had had the feeling that he was being watched for quite some time. He pocketed the note and looked casually round.

It was quite possible that Carter was quite close but keeping very quiet, but he felt it was more likely that they had found a way further up the mountain where it would be impossible to reach them without being seen. His hunch proved correct when, passing through a clearing, he was able to look up at the towering cliff and quite plainly saw a figure looking down at him.

He was tempted to wave at the figure, but he felt that to acknowledge the presence of Hank Carter was, in some way, giving in to him. His feeling was that the longer he ignored Carter, the more frustrated and desperate he would become and therefore more likely to expose himself. It was only human nature as far as Brogan was concerned; Hank Carter was looking for recognition but Brogan was not going to give it to him.

The going did become a little easier in that the frequency of moving rocks and trees became considerably less, in fact for the hour before he was forced to make camp for the night, there were none at all. He even toyed with the idea of travelling on in the dark, but the trail was hazardous enough in daylight so it would be almost impossible in darkness.

Darkness presented Brogan with the opportunity he had been waiting for — to go out and search for Carter. Before leaving, he managed to force a little food and water into the injured man in his charge and, after ensuring that he was well wrapped, he left him asleep on the buckboard.

Unless Hank Carter had qualities Brogan knew nothing of, and he did not believe that to be the case, the odds were all in Brogan's favour. He had many years' experience of this type of terrain, whereas Carter, city bred, had none. Brogan was used to the sounds of the country, Carter was not. More important, Brogan could read and interpret the sounds he did hear and he very much doubted if Carter even really noticed a lot of sounds.

He had seen the lone figure on his right earlier that day, so it seemed perfectly logical that he was still somewhere up there, to his right. Carter had claimed that he was watching and Brogan did not doubt it. It would be important to Carter that his victim knew he was being watched, played with. It was a tactic that Brogan had used himself occasionally in an attempt to wear an opponent down, to force him into a mistake.

Brogan did wonder why Carter had not simply stationed himself somewhere along the trail and waited for his victim to walk into an ambush and this thought began to puzzle him slightly.

There was a good, early moon, and Brogan easily made his way up past the tree line and almost to the top of the cliff. To his surprise, there was quite a well-worn path, obviously either a deer or mountain goat track or possibly both. He followed the track for about a hundred yards before crouching down to look and listen.

The sound was faint, very faint, but it did not escape Brogan's sensitive hearing. It was a cough, possibly human but more than likely a horse. There was a chance that it came from a deer or goat, but there was something about it which told Brogan that it was a horse and that a horse up here could only mean the presence of Hank Carter.

He edged his way further along the narrow animal track only to find that it started to bend, quite sharply, to his left, obviously following the line of a valley or crevasse. The problem was that in doing so, the light of the moon was hidden and he was forced to feel his way knowing that one slip, as had happened, and he had a likely fall of about two hundred feet and he knew that it was most unlikely that he would survive that kind of drop.

He felt the track suddenly start to veer upwards steeply and he had no option but to follow. Quite suddenly he found himself at the top of the cliff and once again able to see around him with the aid of the moonlight. From what he could see, it appeared that he was on a flat piece of ground, perhaps fifty or sixty yards wide, behind which the mountains once again rose steeply.

He heard the cough again, this time very close and he was able to pinpoint the position almost exactly. He crept forward, gun at the ready, listening for other sounds, voices, the shuffling of feet, but there were no such sounds.

He could see the horse plainly enough but that was all there was: one horse, not three as might have been expected and it was certainly not his old horse. There was a saddle and what appeared to be a bedroll alongside the dying embers of a fire, but not a sign of Hank Carter.

Brogan was fairly certain that Carter had not heard him approaching and even if he had heard something, he doubted if he would expect it to be his adversary; he would think it to be some animal. All that though, did nothing to explain why Carter was not there, assuming that he was right and it was Hank Carter and not some other innocent traveller.

To Brogan's mind there was no doubt that the horse did belong to Carter, but the question had to be asked what had happened to Annie and the Irishman and, more importantly at that precise moment, where was Hank Carter himself?

He was forced into the assumption that Carter too had decided to make a night visit to Brogan's camp, which raised the question of why had they not passed or heard each other. Brogan thought back at the noises and odd sounds he had heard, but there was nothing which stood out as having possibly been Hank Carter. In any case, he would have known at the time if it had been.

He had to admit that there was obviously more than one way across and up and down the mountains and that Carter had had the benefit of daylight to assess the ground, so it was almost certain that there was an easier routc. However, the fact of there only being one horse made him realize that Annie had been kept prisoner back along the trail and that the Irishman was guarding her.

Given time, he knew that he would be able to locate Annie and the Irishman, but time was not on his side at that moment; he had an injured man who was getting weaker and would almost certainly die if not seen by a doctor.

He also very seriously considered hiding up and awaiting Carter's return but, although Carter was a greenhorn in the ways of the west and outdoor survival, he realized that he was no fool and was learning rapidly. The main reason against the idea was that it was more than likely that Carter had visited Brogan's camp and he too would realize what had happened, so the chance of Brogan catching Carter unaware was highly unlikely.

"Hell, he might even kill you!" he

muttered to himself. "I guess he's gotta be pretty good to be some kinda shootin' champion."

"There's George to think about too," he reminded himself.

"Yeh, guess so," he sighed. "I feel I kinda owe it to Annie to see that her man gets to a doctor."

"Don't see why the hell you should, she an' him ain't nothin' to you."

"It ain't their fault. That's how I feel anyhow, come on, let's get back. We'll just have to chance meetin' Carter."

"An' if we do?"

"We shoot first!" he grunted.

"Hold on!" he rasped. "I'll let him know we was here!"

He pulled out the note he had found pinned to the signpost and pinned it to the saddle where Carter was sure to find it.

"I reckon that should rattle him a bit!" he said, somewhat pleased with himself.

"Maybe he's left you a note too!" he said.

"Maybe!" he was forced to acknowledge.

It was quite plain that there was at least one more, probably easier way down, but in the dark it would not be the easiest way to find, so he was forced to return the way he had come. It was more than likely that Carter too would return the way he had descended, so the chance of them meeting was remote.

That was exactly how it proved to be. Brogan easily made his way back to camp and found everything as he had left it, except that the fire was almost out. Carter had obviously not searched for anything, nor had he attempted to disturb the injured George. It was not until Brogan had rekindled his fire that he noticed the piece of paper pinned to the side of the buckboard.

I called, you were out!

He was forced to smile and a few moments later he was acknowledging Hank Carter. Carter seemed to have found the note Brogan had left and answered the fact by firing two shots into the air which echoed eerily in the blackness of the valley. Brogan could not resist returning the shots.

He slept easily that night, fairly certain that Carter would not come again. As ever though, his ears were always on the alert, even in sleep.

7

BROGAN was on the move just as dawn broke. He wanted to make Kenton as early as possible and then do what he had to, go and rescue Annie.

The going was much easier; the trail was wider, less rutted and what large obstructions there were were fairly easy to get around. He estimated that it was probably only about ten miles at the most to Kenton, on horseback something over an hour but with the buckboard? He guessed at about four hours without any hold-ups.

There were no hold-ups of the physical kind but the one he had been expecting all along happened after he had been travelling for about two hours.

"I reckon that's about as far as I let you go, McNally!"

151

This observation came after Brogan had rolled off the buckboard in response to a bullet splintering the back rest beside him. He now lay, hidden partly by the buckboard and partly by a rock and clutching his rifle, being forced to listen to the triumphant roar of Hank Carter.

"Lousy shot, Carter!" Brogan called. "Almost killed George instead of me."

"I didn't hit either of you, did I?" came the response. "That's 'cos I didn't intend to."

"I reckon it's 'cos you is a lousy shot!" goaded Brogan.

It was his habit to goad an adversary, especially when he was the one who was pinned down. His reasoning was quite simple; the more agitated a man became, the more mistakes he made. In this instance, he was unsure if Carter had intended to miss or not. If he had, then it had been a very good shot, if he had not then he had to be very grateful for still being alive.

"I don't miss!" shouted Carter. "Certainly not targets as big as a man. Your minutes are numbered, McNally! I'm gonna kill you. I would probably have forgotten all about you leavin' me in that damned desert, I guess I deserved that for tryin' to creep up on you like that. That bank though, that was a different matter. You should've looked after your own business, McNally. I must be honest, I never even gave a thought to you; I sort of assumed you'd passed through a couple of days or so earlier. What kept you?"

It had been difficult to locate Hank Carter precisely and Brogan was quite content to let him talk. All the time he was talking he was not attempting to kill him. He pinpointed the position as being amongst a group of trees on the opposite side of the river, at that point only about twenty feet wide. Brogan had to admit that Carter had chosen well; he now commanded a view and control over the entire valley, which was the narrowest it had been for quite some distance.

Behind Brogan, back along the trail, was a sharp bank down which he had driven and to his left a sheer wall of rock rising to about fifty feet. To his right was the river and attempting to cross would present a very easy target. In front of him was about thirty yards of open ground bounded by sheer rock and the river.

"Horse got lame!" replied Brogan. "Had to rest up."

"It happens!" said Carter. "You wouldn't be in the position you are now if you'd looked after your business though."

"I'd've still found what you did to Annie though; I guess we'd still've been forced together."

"Yeh, pity about her and her old man. Old man! Not much more than a boy. If he'd simply let me and Irish have our way with her, nothin' would have happened to him. But no, he had to play at bein' the good, new husband protecting the honour of his new bride. I know I'm not that old, but I sure as hell wouldn't put my life on the line for the virtue of some woman."

"So where is she now?" urged Brogan, at the same time trying to wriggle towards a large tree stump from where he would be able to get a shot at Carter.

Carter gave a loud laugh. "I don't think so, McNally!" This comment was followed by a shot which grazed Brogan's scalp as it thudded into the ground a few inches in front of his nose. "Now that was intended to split your skull, but I know it hasn't, so don't try an' pretend you're dead."

That had been exactly what Brogan had intended to do, but he realized that city bred though Carter was, he was certainly no fool.

Brogan drew back to the cover of the buckboard and the rock, fully expecting the horse to shy at the shooting and bolt, but the animal appeared very placid and did nothing more than shake its head and flick its tail.

"It's just a matter of time, McNally!" called Carter. "I must admit I wouldn't mind trying to outdraw you, I get the impression that you're no mean hand with a gun."

"Any time!" agreed Brogan.

Carter laughed again. "Sorry, it was just a passing idea, a fancy if you like. The one thing I have learned since I've been out here is that you have to look after number one. I don't know if I could outdraw you or not and I guess I'll never know. We used to have competitions back east to see who was the fastest draw and I won for the last four years. I reckon that doesn't mean a thing out here though. When it's for real it'd be just plain stupid to pit yourself against any man, even a small boy — he might just have the edge and that's the end of you."

"Most killin's are done by shootin' in the back!" said Brogan. "I reckon I can outshoot and outdraw any man, though. If you're half as good as you say you are, I shouldn't be no problem. I'm game if you are. I ain't afraid of dyin'."

"I don't want to die," responded Carter. "Not for a good while yet. I have the impression you mean what you say, about being good and fast and not afraid of dying. It's not being good and fast that scares me, it's the not being scared of dying bit. That makes you a very dangerous man."

"And the longer we keep jawin' the more dangerous I become!" said Brogan, immediately regretting it; it weakened his hand, if he had any to weaken.

"You're right!" called Carter. "I'm going to finish you off."

"Just one thing!" called Brogan. "Why didn't you take me on before this?"

"That's easy!" replied Carter. "There were two of you, I had no idea how good she was with a gun, nor did I know for sure how bad her man was."

"Didn't you come and look for me after I fell?"

"I didn't even know you'd had a fall," said Carter, sounding surprised. "After we took the woman, we didn't hang about. After that, Irish refused to take the risk so I left him with her — I hope he appreciates being left alone with a pretty woman. I suppose I could have killed you anywhere along the trail, but after that little episode in the desert I wasn't too sure. I thought the note was a good idea though."

"Just thought I'd return it," said Brogan.

"Yeh, good job I had the same idea as you. That's enough talkin', your time's up McNally. There's two ways you can die, either stayin' where you are and giving me some target practice or you can try an' make a run for it. Either way you're a dead man."

There was no time for Brogan to reply: three rapid shots from the trees made him huddle behind the large rock. He was realistic enough to know that to show even the top of his head would result in certain death.

There was very little Brogan could do, much to his chagrin, it was not very often that he found himself at such a disadvantage. There was no way of knowing how much ammunition Carter had, but he was quite certain that it was more than enough for the job in hand.

Another shot instantly followed by a sharp pain in his upper arm and Brogan twisted to see that Carter had shifted position, giving him a better view of the rock. Brogan struggled to regain shelter, but another bullet grazed his upper leg.

"Often wondered how it would end!" he hissed to himself. "I guess now I know."

The roar of rifle fire once again echoed around the valley, but this time Brogan felt no impact of a bullet and briefly wondered if he was dead. He suddenly realized that the shooting he could hear now did not come from the rifle or the direction of Hank Carter. The sound of several hoofs clattering on the rocks of the river bed could be plainly heard and, over the general mêlée, Brogan thought he detected the voice of Hank Carter.

"You must have a guardian angel, McNally! Next time I'll kill you!"

A couple of minutes later four riders clattered into view and, on seeing Brogan sprawled behind the rock, surrounded him and took careful aim with their rifles.

"Hold it! Hold it!" Brogan cried. "Can't you see I'm hurt?"

"What the hell's goin' on, Mister?" demanded one of the men who appeared to be the eldest.

"It's a long story," said Brogan, throwing his rifle to one side and trying to get to his feet, which he found a very painful exercise. "Puttin' it briefly, some outlaw called Hank Carter just tried to kill me."

"Hank Carter!" growled the man. "Yeh, I heard of him. There's two

thousand dollars alive on his head."
He peered hard at Brogan. "I ain't
seen no description, but I reckon you
could just as easy be him. Even if you
ain't, I reckon there's a price on your
head."

"My name's McNally, Brogan
McNally." Brogan grinned. "An' I
can assure you there ain't nothin'
on me."

"We heard that one before!" One
of the others growled, spitting an
unhealthy looking black wad on to
the ground. "Who's the feller on the
buckboard?"

"Only name I know is George," said
Brogan. "Is one of you a sheriff or
somethin'?"

They all burst into loud laughter.
"Yeh!" replied the elder man, who
seemed to be the leader. "I guess you
could say we is somethin' like that!"
This was followed by more laughter.

"Bounty hunters!" said Brogan with
a broad grin. "You've gotta be bounty
hunters."

"The best!" said the youngest of the four, proudly. "We heard this Hank Carter feller was around here somewheres; at least he was last seen in some town called Appleby . . . "

"Yeh, that's where I stopped him gettin' away with a load of money from the bank . . . "

"Yeh, we heard somethin' like that too," said the leader. "OK, Mister . . . what you say your name was?"

"McNally, Brogan McNally . . . just call me Brogan."

"Brogan . . . OK, let's hear some sort of explanation."

Brogan sat on the rock and pressed his leg in an attempt to stop the wound bleeding. It did not appear to be too bad.

"I gotta get George here to a doctor!" He indicated the buckboard. "I'm headed for Kenton; they must have a doctor there."

"Hank Carter?" asked one.

"Carter shot him, Carter an' some Irishman."

"Irish?" The leader pulled a wad of papers from his jacket pocket and thumbed through them, stopping occasionally to carefully examine Brogan. He seemed to find what he was looking for. "Irish, real name Paddy McMahon. Small time, only two hundred dollars alive, a hundred dead. OK, I'll buy it that this Hank Carter an' Irish McMahon are here somewheres an' you are who you say you are. Since you seem to know these fellers, you got any idea where they are now, or where they're likely to be?"

"Could be anywhere," said Brogan, dismissively sweeping his arm. He had been going to tell them about Annie, but he resented bounty hunters as a matter of principle, although he had to admit that he was never more grateful to meet one. "I'm a stranger in these parts; just passin' through; a saddle tramp. I found George here an' decided he needed help, so I'm takin' him to Kenton."

"Since when did any saddle tramp

help anyone but himself?" demanded one of them. "An' how d'you know he's called George?"

"He told me," lied Brogan, now resolved that if anyone was going to find Annie and get Hank Carter, it was going to be Brogan McNally and not four evil-looking bounty hunters. "He was conscious when I found him . . . " He grinned widely. "Sides, he offered me a hundred dollars if I'd get him to the doctor."

"That makes more sense, 'specially if he didn't have no money on him," said the leader.

"Both of us seem to be completely broke," Brogan lied again. "Can I go now? If I don't get George here to a doctor alive, I've got no chance of gettin' that hundred dollars."

The four bounty hunters laughed and put their guns away and turned their horses up the trail.

"On your way, McNally," called the leader. "Pity you haven't got a reward out on you, most saddle tramps have,

164

but I can't find nothin' on you. Even if there is it's probably in some State hundreds of miles away an' only a few dollars."

Brogan did not attempt any reply, quite pleased that they were gone. They were the type of men who would rob a man just as easily as they would kill him for the bounty. He patted George and mounted the buckboard, deciding to get to Kenton as quickly as possible both for George's sake and his own. The longer he was in the valley and restricted by the buckboard the more likely he was to be killed by Hank Carter.

Hank Carter had chosen an ideal spot to ambush Brogan; about fifty yards further on the valley widened out again and the trail became level. About two miles further on he came across a homestead and an elderly man leaning on a fence told him that Kenton was about another five miles.

"Who you got there?" wheezed the old man.

"Some feller named George, just moved in with his wife, Annie, some thirty miles up the valley," replied Brogan "He's hurt bad; I gotta get him to a doctor."

"Ain't no doctor in Kenton," wheezed the old man again, this time spitting in the dust. "Leastways not a people doctor. There's Doc Bloom, he's an animal doctor, but they reckon he's pretty good with people too."

"I don't reckon George here is gonna care what kinda doctor it is," said Brogan.

"No, don't reckon he is!" The old man spat again. "I heard about him an' that young wife of his movin' in up there. Don't know what they moved up there for, land ain't fit for nothin' 'ceptin' maybe a few sheep or goats, an' there's already plenty of wild goats up there. What happened?"

"Long story," said Brogan. "Does this Kenton place have a sheriff?"

"Did last time I was there!" The old man spat again. "That was more'n a month ago though; I guess he's still there, I'd've heard if he hadn't been I reckon."

"What's his name?" asked Brogan, urging the horse forward.

"Pete Crawford," replied the old man. "Don't know what you want him for, if there's one thing Pete don't like it's work."

Brogan laughed. "I reckon I've met him before, not that name, but that type of sheriff!"

Despite it having only an animal doctor and a sheriff who did not like work, Kenton turned out to be quite a busy and prosperous looking town, about the same size as Appleby. The veterinarian, Doc Bloom was easy to find and Brogan thought he had better see to George before going to the sheriff.

Doc Bloom examined George still on the buckboard and shook his head. "I ain't so sure as I can handle this. Animals I know what to do with, but people . . . ! We had a proper medical doctor up until a month ago, but the idiot got himself killed when his buggy overturned and broke his neck. Drivin' too fast to a birth they say. OK, I guess I'll just have to see what I can do. Bring him inside."

Brogan unlashed George but, before he carried the limp body inside, he slipped his hand under the body and under George's shirt. He pulled out the money he had been given in Appleby and slipped it into his pocket.

"Thanks for takin' care of it, George," he said, with a grin. "Maybe I'll do the same for you sometime."

Brogan carried George into Doc Bloom's kitchen — he was not equipped with an office to see his patients — where a woman he took to be Mrs Bloom set to ripping George's shirt off.

"What's his name?" asked Doc Bloom.

"I was hopin' you could tell me that," said Brogan. "All I know is he's called George an' he's just newly married with a wife called Annie an' they live way up some valley between here an' Appleby, about thirty-five miles."

"George Watkiss!" announced Mrs Bloom. "I heard they moved in. He married some girl from some bit city somewheres. He's got a brother in town, name of Steve Watkiss."

"Yeh, I heard he had a brother here," said Brogan. "Where do I find him?"

"Workin' in the lumber yard," said Doc Bloom. "He's a foreman or somethin'."

"Thanks, I'll go tell him," said Brogan. "Then I gotta tell the sheriff."

"Pete won't be interested," said Mrs Bloom. "He's not interested in anythin' that happens outside of town."

"He might be interested in what I've got to say," said Brogan.

"I wish you the best of luck!" Mrs Bloom grinned.

The lumber yard was found easily enough, he had passed it on his way into town. A huge water-wheel provided power for saws which could be heard quite plainly. Brogan was directed to a small office at the far end of the yard.

"Steve Watkiss?" asked Brogan of the solitary occupant of the office.

"Who wants to know?" came the unfriendly response.

"It don't matter none who I am," said Brogan. "You have a brother by the name of George?"

"What if I have?"

"I just brought him in from that farm of his," said Brogan. "He's been shot an' he's in a pretty bad way."

"George!" exclaimed Steve Watkiss. "You sure it's George? He only moved in a few weeks ago, just got wed."

"That's another thing," said Brogan. "Seems like a couple of outlaws are holdin' her for some reason."

"Just who the hell are you?" snarled Steve. "You come to try an get some sort of ransom?"

"I'm just a drifter," replied Brogan. "I came across Annie just after two outlaws had raped her an' shot her man. We was bringin' him here when they managed to snatch her again. Don't ask me why they did it, I just don't know. Thing is, he's at Doc Bloom's place right now bein' stitched up or somethin'. That's all I got to say; he's your brother, I done my bit bringin' him here."

Steve Watkiss eyed Brogan warily but finally decided that he was telling the truth. "OK, I'll go see Doc Bloom and ... er ... thanks."

"That's OK," said Brogan. "Now, I'd better go tell this sheriff of yours what's happened."

"Waste of time!" muttered Steve.

"So I been told," Brogan smiled. "All the same, I'll do my duty just so's nobody can say I didn't do nothin'."

Brogan left Steve Watkiss and wandered down the main street until he came across an office which bore the sign 'County Sheriff'. There was a rather rotund man lounging outside who Brogan took to be the sheriff.

"Mornin', Sheriff," said Brogan.

The man looked distastefully at Brogan, sneered slightly and sniffed the air. "Saddle tramp!" he declared. "I smelled you a mile off. I heard you just brought young George Watkiss into town needin' a doctor. What gives?"

Once again Brogan went through the process of explaining what had happened and who the outlaws were, all of which appeared to make very little impression on the sloth-like Sheriff Pete Crawford.

"Don't see as there's much I can do about her," was the rather weary reply. "See, she's out of my territory, I ain't got no jurisdiction out there. Same goes for them outlaws. As long as they keep out there, there ain't nothin' I can do."

"Nothin' you won't do, you mean!" sneered Brogan.

This remark did have some effect in that it forced Crawford to raise his body slightly from the chair he was sitting in and stare hatred at Brogan.

"Listen, bum," snarled Crawford, "I'm sheriff in these parts an' I sure don't need no stinkin' saddle tramp to tell me how to do my job. If they come here I might do somethin', but until then I do nothin'."

"You'd rather leave the dirty work to a bunch of no-good bounty hunters!" goaded Brogan.

"That's the way they earn their livin'," responded Crawford. "If he's out there, they'll find this Hank Carter an' his side-kick. When they do, I'll see to it they get the reward, but I sure ain't breakin' my neck to go lookin'. Hell, you know what it's like out there. There's so many trees you could walk right by a man an' never know he was there."

Brogan had to agree that such a thing was quite likely, especially if it happened to be someone like Sheriff Crawford who was searching.

A couple of minutes later, Steve Watkiss arrived and demanded to know what action the sheriff was going to take and received the same answer Brogan had.

"Told you it'd be a waste of time," Steve said to Brogan as they walked away. "He only keeps the job cos nobody else wants it."

"So what are you gonna do?" asked Brogan. "She is your sister-in-law."

"Me?" Steve nodded horrified at the suggestion. "Hell, what can I do? I ain't never set eyes on the woman. She's only kin by marriage an' I've got my own wife an' family to think about. I know my Mary wouldn't take kindly to me riskin' my life tryin' to rescue someone we ain't never met."

"She is your brother's wife!" Brogan pointed out.

"That ain't no problem of my doin'!" insisted Steve. "I did try to talk him out of livin' out there an marryin' a city girl. It'll never work, he should've married a country girl; they is used to that kind of life."

"So as far as you're concerned she

can stay out there an' be raped an' murdered."

"Who's to say she ain't been murdered already?"

Brogan shook his head. He had to agree; who was to say she was still alive?

8

IT had been a long time since
Brogan had ridden bareback, in
fact he could not remember the
last occasion. Now, however, he had
little alternative but to use that most
insecure means of travel since his own
horse and saddle had been spirited
away whilst he was sleeping under
the trees.

Strictly speaking, the horse was not
his, it belonged to George Watkiss but,
since George was hardly in a position
to argue the matter, Brogan unhitched
the animal from the buckboard and led
it out of town. He did not ride it, just
in case he fell off, and he did not fancy
making a spectacle of himself.

He had, tentatively, enquired the
price of a saddle but either they were
genuinely dearer than he imagined or
someone was trying to prise as much

money away from him as they could. He decided that it was more than likely the latter, having had quite considerable experience of human nature.

Doc Bloom had suggested that Brogan pay for the treatment he had given George, to which Brogan responded by suggesting that it was a family matter. If Sheriff Crawford was surprised to see Brogan heading out of town in the direction he had come, he did not show it, nor did he truly care. He was just thankful to be rid of a potential troublemaker.

Fortunately for Brogan, the horse was a very placid animal, in many ways very much like his own. Like her, she seemed to have two speeds — slow and stop — and like her she seemed to respond to his talking in much the same way. Unlike his own horse however, she was a draught horse and not a riding horse and was that much bigger. After a very short time he felt as though he was splitting up the middle as his legs were forced apart by the broad back of the animal. Despite this, he did manage to stay on her back.

He passed the same homestead on the way out as on the way in and it seemed to him that the same old man was in exactly the same position and chewing on the same, unlit pipe.

"Find the doc?" asked the old man.

"An' the sheriff," said Brogan, not attempting to stop. "You was right about that sheriff, he didn't want to know anythin'."

"What you goin' back that way for?" asked the old man."

"Annie's out there somewhere," replied Brogan. "I feel kinda responsible for her; she's been taken by a couple of outlaws."

"Be better for her if them bounty hunters don't catch her!"

Brogan was a few yards past the old man, but this time he did stop the horse. "What you know 'bout them?" he demanded.

"Almost everybody knows about Greasy Speak an' his cronies," responded the old man. "Leastwise everyone in these parts does. They is one reason Pete Crawford ain't bothered. If they have a reward out on 'em, he leaves it to Greasy to bring 'em in. I reckon they give him a cut. I'd watch out for them four if I was you, mister, they is worse'n most the men they bring in. If they find this Annie you can be sure they'll have their way with her an they'll kill anyone who gets in their way. You met up with 'em? I'd say you was lucky; they is just as liable to kill the likes of you as spit on the ground." He stressed the point by depositing a liberal wad of unsavoury matter from his mouth on to the ground.

"Yeh, I met 'em," Brogan nodded. "I know the type. OK, I'll be on the lookout."

"Take a tip from an old stager, mister," offered the old man. "Don't sleep out in the open an' don't be sweet talked if one or two of 'em stop you, the other two'll be close behind, ready to put a bullet in your back."

"I reckon they know this country?" said Brogan.

"Greasy was born an' raised here," the old man grinned. "He's some sort of kin of mine, I ain't sure just how an' I ain't too proud of it."

"An' all that up there is just one big ambush!" said Brogan. He thought for a moment. "I got me an idea. How about you lookin' after this horse? She's one hell of an uncomfortable ride; I reckon I'd be better on foot."

"Now you're talkin' like a true woodsman," grinned the old man. "Sure, take her round the back, she can run in the paddock with mine." He made no attempt to move either as Brogan turned and rode through the open gate or as he let her loose in the paddock.

"Another thing," said the old man as Brogan started out on foot. "Keep to the high ground if you can, they won't be expectin' that."

"Thought they was kin of yours?" said Brogan.

"So one of 'em is. That don't mean I have to like 'em though."

Brogan gave a brief wave and continued his walk. It was a long way, especially since he did not know where Annie was being kept, but even if he had to walk all the way back to the farm, it would probably be quicker than with the buckboard.

He ignored the old man's advice to keep to the high ground, partly because it would have made progress that much slower and partly through stubborn pride. He maintained that he could detect trouble long before it arrived. He had to admit that he had been wrong about Hank Carter and being ambushed.

"That was 'cos I was drivin' that damned buckboard!" he declared to himself. "How's a feller expected to hear anythin' drivin' one of them things?"

There were many signs of people and horses being passed in both directions; the ones he had made driving the buckboard were easy to detect and much older tracks were easy to distinguish. What he did not know was the frequency of traffic, although he thought that it was not all that frequent. From a fairly jumbled start, he soon picked up what he thought were the tracks of the four bounty hunters.

He wanted to know where the four were, not to tackle them but to avoid them. However, since they seemed to be well versed in the country and were looking for Hank Carter, it was more than likely that their tracks would lead to Carter, although he would have liked to have reached Carter before they did.

Some time later he came to the spot where Carter had ambushed him and, noting that the bounty hunters had carried on up stream, he crossed and examined the ground among the clump of trees. He succeeded in finding clear signs of Carter having ridden out in a hurry, the trail at first disappearing into the river and re-emerging about sixty yards upstream to lead up a very narrow, very high-sided almost tunnel-like crevasse.

There was barely enough room to get a horse along, and he had serious doubts if he would have been able to get the draught horse up it. However, the signs were still there, quite clear. Brogan began to marvel at Carter's ingenuity and rapid grasp of the ways of the west.

After about half a mile, the floor of the crevasse began to rise, at first quite gradually but quite steeply towards the end. The end came as Brogan found himself on a ledge, about twenty yards wide and seemingly fairly flat, twisting around the mountains in both directions. There were quite clear signs of someone having taken the same route fairly recently. A single set of tracks, which meant that the bounty hunters were not yet up at this level, at least not at that point.

Brogan was certain that Greasy Speak would not be long in finding his way up, especially since he apparently knew the area better than anyone. He shrugged; Greasy and his cronies were just another problem he might have to deal with. He would have preferred not to cross the bounty hunters, but he had this distinct feeling that that was not to be.

The tracks he was following led off to his right across very rocky ground and it was evident that Hank Carter, assuming he was following Carter's tracks, had had to dismount and lead his horse. The going was fairly easy for a man on foot and it certainly made progress less conspicuous and offered plenty of hiding places in case of trouble.

As he slowly made his way along, he kept quite close to the edge so that he could keep a constant eye on the trail snaking along the valley some two hundred feet below. He did wonder how Hank Carter had known of this wide ledge, for that was all it was in reality, but he did not tax his mind too much about it; he had to admit that it had given Carter the advantage.

The further he progressed, the narrower the ledge became, until eventually it was no more than three feet wide in places. There did not appear to be any way of climbing higher with a horse, the side was sheer all the way. However, should he find it necessary, it offered quite an easy climb.

The signs were still quite plain, Hank had passed this way, for the most part leading his horse but, as yet, he had seen no sign of Greasy Speak. Darkness came without any sign of anyone and Brogan found a convenient overhang under which to shelter for the night.

Any idea of lighting a fire was completely out of the question and Brogan was resigned to a cold night. He did not have any blankets or bedroll so all he could do was huddle against a large rock which shielded him from the prevailing wind.

As ever, conditioned by years of sleeping out in the open, Brogan's senses were on the alert and it must have been about two hours after nightfall that he heard them.

Making his way to the edge, he looked down into the blackness that was the valley and river. At first he could see nothing, although there were clear signs that someone was moving about below him. Suddenly a flame split the darkness as a fire was lit. Brogan shivered slightly, the flames looked very warm and inviting.

Shapes were indistinct, but he detected four of them and, although he had only spoken to them once, he recognized the voices of the bounty hunters. It was impossible to make out what they were talking about and it did not matter to him. Now at least he knew where the opposition was and he liked to know things like that.

Actually, the presence of the bounty hunters told Brogan quite a lot. He was reasonably certain that they had travelled at least as far as the farm belonging to Annie and George and it was obvious that they had found nothing, so that saved Brogan the trouble of going to the farm himself. It also told him that unless the bounty hunters had found and killed Hank Carter, Carter was almost certainly not down on the floor of the valley.

Brogan looked along the darkness of the ledge and toyed with the idea of continuing in the hope that Carter or the Irishman had a fire. He thought about it and then decided against it. It was very dark and there was always the chance that he might slip and go over the edge and he had had enough of things like that just lately. He retired to his cold shelter.

* * *

Brogan was peering over the edge just as dawn broke but it was about half an hour later before any of the bounty hunters below stirred themselves. The fire was rekindled and a pot of water placed on it to make coffee. Brogan was not a great coffee drinker, but at that precise moment the thought of a good, hot, strong coffee was most inviting.

The night had been very cold, although he had spent colder and more uncomfortable nights and where he was there was not even a pool of water to drink. He licked his lips and kept watch on the movements below.

After their coffee — they did not bother with anything to eat — the fire was doused and the men rode off back down the valley. Brogan just wished that he had some idea what their next move was going to be. However, he now knew which direction they were going and where they might come from but his prime object was still to find Annie.

He had already decided that should he be able to rescue Annie, the fate of Hank Carter or the Irishman would be the least of his worries. If they got away he was not going to try and follow them. If he was forced into a showdown then he would face up to that. Either way, he was not at all interested in what became of Hank Carter.

He continued along the ledge for about an hour when he came upon the first real signs of the recent presence of Carter. It seemed that he had camped the previous night in a small hollow and had felt safe enough to light a fire. Brogan decided that he was probably unaware that he was being followed by him or the subject of interest to the bounty hunters.

The embers of the fire, although cold, were not damp, as would have been the case had the fire been older than the previous night. Carter was still leading his horse, which was bound to slow him down quite considerably. Riding a horse along the now very narrow ledge was very dangerous.

About half an hour later, he suddenly heard the snort of a horse and the not-so-quiet cursing of Hank Carter. Ensuring that he was not seen, Brogan crept forward and, peering around the edge of quite a sharp bend, he could see Carter trying to persuade his horse to negotiate a particularly large rock which almost completely blocked the ledge.

A man could quite easily get by, either by skirting the rock or by climbing over it, but a horse was a very different matter. Carter had negotiated the rock and was now attempting to pull the frightened animal around it. As far as Brogan could tell, the rock must have fallen quite recently, probably since Carter had negotiated the trail, but it appeared to be too big for one man to man-handle over the edge.

It took about half an hour, but the horse was eventually coaxed around the rock, although one slip would have sent the animal falling over two hundred feet. Brogan was more concerned for the horse than he was for Carter.

Brogan suddenly realized that as Carter carried on along the ledge, he had only to look back and he was almost certain to see him. He looked along the ledge and could see no suitable cover, so he had no alternative but to retreat almost a hundred yards until he was out of sight. That was when he encountered his second problem.

On the ledge, on the other side of a large, 'V' shaped sweep, two of the bounty hunters were slowly making their way on foot. A quick glance below showed him that the other two were following the trail with the other two horses. Brogan managed to hide behind an outcrop of rock until the two men on the opposite side of the 'V' were far enough along not to be able to see him and the two below had temporarily been hidden from view. He rapidly made his way back towards Hank Carter, to find that he had disappeared around another corner. At that moment he would rather have faced Hank Carter than the bounty hunters. The two on the ledge would have been easy to deal with, but he knew that the two down on the trail would soon locate him and probably kill him.

The rock that had caused Carter so much trouble was easily crossed and the next corner reached. He had to reach the safety of the corner as quickly as possible since he was once again in clear view of his followers.

Carter was now about fifty or sixty yards ahead and, with little in the way of cover, all Brogan could do was to crouch low and hope he was not seen.

Hank Carter seemed distinctly uneasy and looked behind several times. Brogan had sensed the unease and did not relish the idea of being trapped between the outlaw and the bounty hunters. Neither would be too bothered about shooting an ageing saddle tramp who happened to be in the way. There had been only one thing he could do and that was take the one slim chance he had and climb upwards.

His only chance came in the form of a very narrow recess which afforded some cover from the view of Carter and the following bounty hunters. From the trail, however, he was still in full view although luck seemed to be with him as the two bounty hunters on the trail did not bother to look up.

By the time Brogan had reached a small shelf which afforded complete cover from below, the two bounty hunters on the ledge had rounded the corner and were confronting Hank Carter. However, Carter had prepared himself and he did not give either man the opportunity to do or say anything.

Carter had found cover behind the only thing on the ledge which gave him any cover — his horse. The two bounty hunters were obviously taken completely unawares as Carter's first and very accurate shot drilled a hole clear in the centre of the forehead of the leading bounty hunter. Carter's second shot was not quite so accurate, but it was nonetheless very effective in slamming into the back of the other bounty hunter and sending him flying over the two-hundred-foot drop. The shot had not killed him, but the fall certainly did. The first man's body had also fallen over the edge, but he had been very dead before he fell.

There was a flurry of shots from below as the two remaining bounty hunters raced to get a clear view of Carter and, from his hiding place, Brogan was forced to smile since he knew that the bounty hunters were wasting their ammunition, Carter was at the extreme range of their rifles.

It seemed that Carter too realized that he was out of effective range and simply laughed loudly, which echoed all around the valley. There was an answering echo from below as Greasy bellowed his vengeance. Brogan was quite happy to look and listen.

Greasy Speak did not make any attempt to go after Hank Carter, he knew the area well enough to realize that it would be impossible to get at the man, but he also knew that Hank Carter was trapped. All he had to do was watch and wait.

This fact was not lost on Brogan and he needed Carter to be able to continue and lead him to Annie and the Irishman. Greasy Speak and his companion had disappeared, leaving behind the two spare horses and Brogan knew that they had moved further up the trail to take up positions closer to Carter, so unless the outlaw knew of some other way, he was trapped. Even if he decided to go back, one man strategically placed would soon kill him. He decided, a little against his better judgement, that he had no alternative but to help Carter.

With the departure of the men on the trail, climbing down was not a problem and he found another, fairly easy way, from the ledge down to the trail where he collected one of the spare horses. Although he had decided that Carter needed help, Brogan had no idea what exact form that help was going to take. It was against his nature to simply ride up to a man and shoot him; it was something he had never had to do and did not intend doing now. He would kill a man in a fair fight and think nothing of it, but he doubted if even he, hard as he was, had the stomach for pure murder.

He rode slowly along the valley, fully expecting one or both bounty hunters to challenge him at any moment. There was little information to be gleaned from the activities of the wildlife or birds since there had been more than enough happening to scare off any deer or goats and most of the birds had long since flown away.

After five minutes Brogan was more than surprised not to have been challenged or even shot at, but there was not even a sign or sound of their horses. It was obvious that Greasy Speak had some other plan in mind. He decided to return along the trail and keep a check on the progress of Hank Carter.

He knew he had passed the point where he had climbed down to the trail, the remaining horse was about a hundred yards back, grazing contentedly, but Brogan had not seen any sign of Hank Carter. He returned along the trail and then back again, but still the ledge above was completely devoid of life. It was as though Hank Carter had been spirited away.

Brogan once again followed the sheer wall of rock, this time concentrating on looking for possible ways down, but there were none and neither were there any signs that both Carter and his horse had fallen. Brogan was quite certain such a thing had not happened, he would have heard any such fall, just as he would have heard any gunfire if Greasy Speak had found him.

"OK!" Brogan said to himself. "So there's either some way up or there's somewheres he can hide up."

"So what you gonna do?" he replied.

"Go up there again, I guess!"

"You gotta be crazy! You think them bounty hunters is gonna bother who you is, they'll just shoot."

"Maybe," he agreed. "You got any better ideas?"

"Yeh, sure have, get the hell out of here, right now!"

"That'd make sense," he had to agree. "Only trouble is, when did we ever do anythin' that was sense?"

"Not often! OK, make your mind up!"

Brogan had already made his mind up. He left the horse with the other one and made his way to the rock face.

9

THE climb was easy enough and there was still no sign of the bounty hunters, a fact which did bother him slightly, although they were the last people he wanted to see at that moment. For the climb, he had to strap his rifle to his back, using a piece of rope he had found in the saddle-bag of the bounty hunter's horse. It made climbing a little more difficult, but he was eventually at the top.

Hank Carter's tracks were plain to see although there was no question of following the wrong ones on such a narrow ledge. The ledge suddenly entered a deep crevasse and at first seemed to double back on itself on the other side but, at what seemed to be a dead end, he found another, narrower crevasse off to the left. It was just about wide enough for a horse to be led along and, after a few yards, it started to climb steadily upwards.

Once again the signs were very clear, a man and horse had passed through very recently. From that point onwards, Brogan was on his guard, he had no idea what lay ahead or where Hank Carter was. It was quite possible that Carter was waiting somewhere ahead for anyone who dared to follow.

As it happened, the end of the crevasse was reached without sign of Carter and Brogan heaved a sigh of relief as he warily peered out of the hole into a very narrow, steep-sided valley. There was only one way Carter could have gone and that was straight along the narrow valley.

The rough scree on either slope, rising about four or five hundred feet, was bleak and offered no foothold but, more importantly from Brogan's point of view, no boulders large enough to hide a horse.

The floor of the valley rose steadily and was quite obviously a regular water course as it drained off the surrounding mountains, although at that moment it was completely dry. That explained the crevasse; the water, when in full flow, had to go somewhere.

There was still no sighting of Hank Carter, although there were plenty of indications of him having passed that way but Brogan realized that it could not be long before Carter reached the place where the Irishman and Annie were, if they were still alive. As ever, Brogan's senses were alert to every sound.

The sound did not come from ahead, it quite definitely came from behind and since he was still following signs made by Carter, he had to assume that Greasy Speak and his remaining crony had finally picked up the trail and were now close behind.

Brogan hid behind a large rock and looked back down the narrow valley which ran almost straight. For a couple of minutes there was no sign or sound but he suddenly detected a movement among the rocks about half a mile away. There were two figures, as expected, but no horses. Brogan was reasonably certain that he had not been seen but once again he was trapped and was certain to be shot at by both parties. He decided to move upwards about fifty or sixty feet behind a large boulder.

From the shelter of his rock, Brogan was able to see further along the valley, which at that point flattened out slightly and, about half a mile further on, he could see three horses, one of which he recognized, even from that distance, as his old horse. At first he did not see anything else except the horses, but a slight movement a few yards away pinpointed two of the three.

One was quite definitely Annie and Brogan assumed that the other was the Irishman simply because it did not look like Hank Carter. At first there was no sign of Carter but suddenly he was directly below, crouching behind a rock and looking back along the valley. It was quite obvious that he had seen

Greasy Speak approaching.

Brogan half expected Carter to climb up to his rock, but he did not, instead racing back to the others. After an animated conversation with the Irishman, it appeared that Annie was tied up and the two men dispersed one either side of the camp. There was no attempt to hide the horses and Brogan wondered if this was an oversight or planned strategy — lulling the bounty hunters into believing that their approach had not been seen.

Brogan glanced up at the sky and noted that there was only about one hour to go before sunset. He was slightly surprised, time seemed to have passed very quickly. He had not eaten that day, which was nothing unusual, but his throat was parched, a drink of water would have been more than welcome.

The bounty hunters were now almost directly below him and it would have been an easy task to kill both of them but his conscience would not allow him to kill in cold blood; besides, it was more than possible that Carter and the Irishman would do that job quite well.

The bounty hunters stopped and Greasy Speak pointed in the direction of the horses and both men crouched low, whispering to each other and occasionally pointing. Brogan was willing them to move towards the camp but it seemed that Greasy was either not so easily fooled or had other ideas. Brogan saw him look up at the sky and could almost read the bounty hunter's thoughts: he was going to wait until after nightfall. Brogan began to wish that it was nightfall already, he was very cramped and with all the loose scree about, there was a danger that even the slightest movement would send loose stones cascading down the hillside. All he could do was wait.

He had to admit that it was an interesting situation and he would dearly have liked to have witnessed the outcome but the impending darkness and the preoccupation of the men below with each other had given Brogan an idea.

The situation below was almost farcical: it was quite plain that both sets of men knew of the presence of the other, but neither seemed willing to admit as much, almost fooling themselves into believing that each held the element of surprise. Brogan did not mind; while they were concentrating on each other, neither would think that anyone else was around.

There was virtually no movement from either sets of men until darkness began to close in and then the bounty hunters started to ease closer. Brogan waited until it was completely dark before he made his move, creeping slowly from behind his rock and slowly making his way upwards. He had taken the opportunity to memorize almost every stone between him and the camp where Annie was, noting a ridge of firmer ground which swept round behind the camp. What was happening between the others was now of secondary importance, his object was to get Annie away.

It took him a little over ten minutes to circle behind the camp and there he paused for a time, waiting for some action.

A single shot from nearby shattered the quiet and was answered by a volley of shots from further away. The shooting continued for some time and Brogan swiftly made his way down to where Annie was tied up. He clamped his hand across her mouth and whispered to her.

"Not a sound!" he urged. "It's me, Brogan. Hold still while I cut these ropes."

Annie obediently lay quiet as Brogan cut the ropes and then threw her arms around his neck unable to control her sobs.

"I never thought I'd be so glad to see anyone!" she choked.

"Save your gratitude for later!" whispered Brogan. "Right now we've got to get you away from here. Now do exactly what I say, no questions, just do everythin' I tell you."

"How . . . how . . ."

"I said, no questions!" Brogan hissed. "Now, take a hold of my hand an' follow me."

She obediently took his hand and followed him up the quite steep slope behind the camp. As they climbed there was a shout from Greasy Speak to Hank Carter.

"You've got no chance!" came the call. "If you want the chance to live, give yourselves up!"

"Not a hope!" yelled Carter in reply. "You'll never find us!"

"We can wait!" replied Greasy. "We know this valley; you're in a box; there ain't nowhere you can go. Even if there was, you'd never be able to take your horses an' after that it'd just be a matter of time 'fore we caught you."

"I wouldn't be too sure of that!" called Carter. "If the two men I killed earlier were anythin' to do with you,

you must know that."

"Sure, we know that," shouted Greasy. "Two good men, I oughta kill you for killin' them, but you is worth more alive. The choice is yours, Carter, give yourselves up an' there's a chance you might live, otherwise we'll be quite happy to take the reward for you dead, that's still a thousand."

"Go shit!" called Carter.

Brogan and Annie had taken advantage of the commotion to climb the scree without taking too much care and stop briefly on a patch of level ground to catch their breath.

"I ain't got the faintest idea where we're goin'," he panted. "I guess all we can do is keep movin', we'll find a way out eventually. Let's just hope they is occupied long enough not to realize you is gone."

"What do you think they'll do when they do find out?" she asked.

"Probably nothin'," replied Brogan. "Come on, let's put as much distance between them an' us as we can."

★ ★ ★

Hank Carter realized that he was boxed in, but he was a resourceful man and decided that attack was the one thing the bounty hunters would not be expecting. He silently crossed to where the Irishman was hidden.

"OK, Mister Carter," said Irish, "this was your bright idea, what do we do now?"

"We kill 'em!" hissed Carter.

"Just like that!" Irish laughed quietly. "Easy, the man says, we just kill 'em. Tell me, just how the hell are we gonna do that? It's pitch dark, I almost shot you just then thinkin' it was one of them. OK, I'm all ears, I guess I can't be no worse off dead than I am now."

"You draw their fire," instructed Carter. "Move around a bit so they can't pinpoint you and it'll make them think we're both still here."

"An' just where will you be?"

"While they're shootin' at you, I'll

be able to tell where they are," Carter pointed out. "It'll be me who's takin' the risk: I've got to get close enough to kill them."

"Personally I'm all for givin' up," said Irish. "I know I'm due for a long time in prison, but I haven't done a hangin' offence."

"Is that what you really want?" asked Carter.

"No, I guess not," admitted Irish. "OK, I'll draw their fire, you go do your damnedest."

Hank Carter melted into the darkness and a short time afterwards Irish started shooting. One of his shots must have been fairly close as one of the bounty hunters cursed loudly and responded by shooting back, followed by shooting from the other.

As instructed, Irish moved around as Carter gradually closed in. It did not take him long to locate one of them and, in the almost total darkness, he could just make out a shape behind a rock. His shot was true to his boast of being an excellent marksman and the man gave a brief grunt as he slumped.

"Carl!" came the cry from Greasy. "Carl! Are you all right?"

"Carl's dead!" Carter could not help but proclaim the fact. "That leaves just you, whoever you are. Prepare to die!"

This time it was Greasy Speak who realized that he had underestimated his opposition and was wise enough to know that on his own he stood little chance.

Irish continued shooting for some time, but he was unable to draw any fire and eventually Carter realized that the man must have fled. He could not help but congratulate himself on a job well done.

"Hold your fire, Irish!" he called. "I reckon the bird's flown the coop!"

There was a brief pause before Irish replied. "Thank goodness for that!" he said eventually. "I was beginning to get worried."

"One of 'em's dead!" announced Carter. "I don't know who they were, but they seemed to know who I was."

"If it's any consolation, Mr Carter," said Irish. "I think every one in every state must know who you are."

"Maybe so," agreed Carter, actually quite proud of the fact. "You've been around here for quite a time, have you any idea who this one is?"

Irish joined him as he lit a match to light up the scene. Irish grunted and turned the man over.

"Did I hear the other one call him Carl?" he said.

"That's what he said!" agreed Carter.

"Then this one is Carl Nixon. I reckon the other one must have been Greasy Speak. Bounty hunters! Four of them there were but since you've accounted for three of 'em, I guess that just leaves Greasy. Greasy on his own is bad enough; he's a real mean character."

"Bounty hunters!" grunted Carter. "I guess that explains it. Don't worry about the one called Greasy; he won't be no trouble from now on."

"I wouldn't be too certain of that!" warned Irish.

"Well, I don't think we'll get any more problems from him tonight," assured Carter. "Let's go tell the woman they hadn't come to rescue her."

They returned to the camp and found only the cut ropes that had bound their hostage. Immediately both were on the alert, holding their rifles at the ready.

"This was no accident," announced Irish. "She didn't cut these ropes by herself, someone's been here!"

"Don't tell me the obvious!" snarled Carter. "Four bounty hunters you said. I've killed three of them and the other is hightailin' it out of here . . . " He suddenly laughed. "McNally!" He laughed again. "Yeh, it's got to be McNally, there's nobody else with any reason to be up here!" He suddenly called out at the top of his voice. "OK,

McNally, you've got the woman back, for all the good it's goin' to do you. I must admit, you've got one hell of a nerve but I'll get you I can promise you that! Keep goin', McNally, keep runnin', it's your only chance!"

The message echoed around the blackness of the mountains and in the distance Brogan smiled.

"What's it between you and this McNally?" asked Irish. "If you think I'm followin' you around the country lookin' for him, you're mistaken."

"He's interfered once too often!" Carter laughed again. "Please yourself what you do, Irish, nobody's forcin' you to do anythin' you don't want to."

"If you had any sense," said Irish, "you'd forget about him and get to Canada or Mexico like you said. That sounded like a good idea to me."

"I'll get there!" asserted Carter. "Don't you worry none about that!"

"I do worry!" muttered Irish.

"What I'd like to know is how the

hell he got up here without bein' seen either by them or us," said Carter.

"Maybe he's thrown in with them," said Irish.

"McNally? No, he's a loner; he wouldn't get involved with nobody else," said Carter. "His trouble is he's got a noble streak in him and can't keep his nose out of trouble."

"Then let someone else chop his nose off!" said Irish. "Make your mind up what you want to do, Mr Carter. I'll stay with you if we head for Canada or Mexico, but I am not chasin' all over the country on any personal vendetta of yours."

Carter laughed again and slapped Irish across the shoulder. "You're right!" he admitted. "We can't afford the luxury of going after him. I reckon every lawman in the country will be looking for us now."

"Yeh, that's another thing I'm worried about!" muttered Irish.

★ ★ ★

Brogan listened intently and was eventually satisfied that they were not being followed. He had found a small cave and, after deciding that it was safe enough, he told Annie to get some sleep. It was a bitterly cold night but he felt safe enough to light a fire.

"How did you find me?" asked Annie. It had been the first opportunity she had had to question Brogan.

"Just followed a few tracks," replied Brogan, blandly.

"That simple!" she said, slightly incredulous.

"That simple," said Brogan. "It must've been simple for them bounty hunters to follow him too."

"Is that what they were?" she said. "I thought it was the sheriff or somebody."

"Sheriff!" Brogan laughed. "It takes that sheriff all his time an' effort to get out of his chair." He looked at Annie in the glow of the fire. "Are you all right, did they hurt you at all?"

"Only my pride this time," she replied. "The Irishman was quite nice really, even if he did rape me before. This time neither of them laid a finger on me."

"Glad to hear it," said Brogan, with genuine feeling.

"George!" said Annie. "What happened to him, is he all right?"

"He was bein' seen to when I left him," said Brogan. "I left him with Doc Bloom in Kenton. I managed to find his brother an' tell him what had happened."

"Didn't they organize a posse?"

"To be honest, nobody, includin' your old man's brother, didn't seem interested," said Brogan. "Maybe I just caught 'em on the wrong foot though."

"Steve would have done something if he could," said Annie, more to convince herself than Brogan. "I'm certain of it."

"Yeh, I guess he would," agreed Brogan.

10

BROGAN was up at dawn but he allowed Annie to sleep on. He spent the next half-hour hunting for something to eat and looking for water. The water was no problem, there was a clear pool about fifty yards from the cave, but food proved a little more elusive. He did sight a deer, but she sensed him first and bolted. A jack-rabbit caught him unawares and had disappeared by the time he raised his rifle. In the end he managed to trap a couple of large lizards which were cooking over the fire when Annie awoke.

"Mmmm . . . that smells good!" she enthused. "I'm starving."

"Tastes good too," assured Brogan.

"Lizard!" exclaimed Annie in a horrified voice. Brogan turned to see her holding up the skins of the lizards.

"You don't expect me to eat lizard do you?"

"It's either lizard or you go hungry," said Brogan. "Try some, it's quite good really."

"Ugh!" grimaced Annie, throwing the offending skins away. She sniffed the air again. "I must admit that they don't smell at all bad." She prodded the offering Brogan gave her impaled on a stick and gingerly bit into it. Very slowly her expression changed from one of apprehension and horror to almost pleasure. "Hey, they're not too bad!"

"Never call somethin' until you try it, I always say," said Brogan. "I did try for rabbit or deer, but I couldn't get near enough."

"So what do we do now?" she asked.

"We go back!" he announced.

"Back!" she exclaimed in alarm.

"Yeh, back," said Brogan. "If you is thinkin' it was you I came for, you is wrong. The one female in my life is still back there — my horse!"

Annie pulled a face and bit hard on the lizard tail. "It's nice to think I come second to some horse!"

"A horse is a whole lot more use to a man like me than any woman!" Brogan was smiling and she pulled a face at him, although she was not quite sure if he was teasing her or not.

"Maybe they'll've taken your damned horse with them," she mumbled as she chewed.

"Shouldn't think so," said Brogan. "The horses they got are a whole lot better'n mine, younger an fitter anyhow. They've probably just turned her loose. Can't see 'em even botherin' with my saddle; it's a bit battered an' old, but it suits me."

"Damned uncomfortable it was!" she grinned. "OK, I don't suppose I have much choice."

"Not a lot," agreed Brogan. "You could always start walkin' if you want."

"If I knew where I was, I might," she replied. "For the moment I think I'd be better sticking with you."

Brogan doused the fire and they set off the way they had come. There was no chance of getting lost, their tracks from the previous night were quite plain.

Travelling in daylight more than halved the time it had taken in the dark and, less than an hour later, they were looking down on the site where the camp had been. As expected, Hank Carter and the Irishman had gone, but until that moment Brogan had not known for sure what to expect. He had heard Hank Carter shout the previous night, and he had formed the opinion that Carter had probably beaten off the bounty hunters. Seeing the body of Carl Nixon more or less confirmed what he already thought.

"Shouldn't we take him with us?" said Annie, shuddering slightly at the sight of the fly-infested body.

"Naw!" said Brogan, blandly. "Buzzards gotta eat too!" He went over to his horse, who tossed her head and neighed as he approached. "Stupid great lump!"

Brogan scolded as he patted her neck. "I thought you an' me was buddies. What you wanna let some stranger take you away for? Hell it comes to somethin' when I can't even trust my own horse." She gave a loud neigh and shook her head.

Annie was looking at them both almost bemused. "You don't think she understands what you're saying do you?"

"Every word!" assured Brogan. "I'm beginnin' to wonder if I shouldn't trade you in for a younger one though." The effect of this remark was for her to toss her head and knock Brogan over. "See what I mean about her knowin' every word!" he grinned.

Annie's belief that animals could not understand was slightly shaken. "It sure seems she does," she had to agree.

Brogan's saddle was still there, along with what few belongings he had. His money was in his shirt pocket and he transferred it to a special pouch hidden under the saddle. After saddling his horse, he pulled Annie up behind him and they started off.

"You're serious about leaving that man here, aren't you?" she said, slightly horrified.

"It ain't gonna make no difference to him," said Brogan. "'Sides, we ain't got room for another passenger. Sure, we leave him, in a couple of days all that'll be left is bones."

Annie shuddered. "I wouldn't like to think that I'd just been left like that. I think we ought to bury him at least."

"Won't make no difference!" said Brogan. "Look over there!" He nodded up the slope behind them. "Wolf! Lone female by the looks of it, probably got some cubs somewheres near. They ain't usually carrion eaters, but if she's got cubs an' can't hunt too well, she'll take anythin'." He glanced into the sky. "Buzzards!" He pointed. "I've seen buzzards pull the earth off a grave before now. No, he's best left where he is. Maybe you can tell somebody when you get to Kenton. Just tell 'em he was one of the bounty hunters."

Annie shuddered again and gripped Brogan tightly round the waist. "I hate buzzards! Come on, let's get out of here, I don't want to witness any of them feeding."

It took about another hour to reach the point where the crevasse started and Brogan made Annie and his horse wait at the top while he silently made his way down. The crevasse was an ideal place for an ambush and, although he did not really expect one, he was not prepared to take the chance. Half an hour later he was back with Annie assuring her that the way ahead was clear.

"I think this is the way I was brought in," she said. "I seem to recognize the place."

"Just about the only way in an' out with a horse as far as I can see," said Brogan.

"Are you expecting trouble?" she asked.

"I always expect trouble," said Brogan,

"that way I'm never surprised when it comes. Maybe Carter an' the Irishman have decided to get the hell out of it, but I wouldn't bank on it. Seems as how Carter's got a grudge against me."

Brogan found that he had to walk in front of his horse, not so much to lead her down the narrow crevasse but to help stop her from sliding down the steep, slippery slope. Smooth rock did not give a very secure foothold for either human or animal and a couple of times it took all of Brogan's strength wedging himself against the rock to prevent his horse slipping. Eventually they reached more level rock as the crevasse joined the other, larger crevasse. From that point onwards the going was quite easy, hampered only by the narrowness of the ledge.

"We came in the other way," said Annie as she walked behind Brogan and the horse. "It didn't seem so narrow. I'm terrified of heights!" She kept as close to the rock face as possible and refused to look down into the valley unless she had to.

"Ain't nothin' to be scared of bein' high," said Brogan, laughingly. "It's when you fall you got trouble."

"Thanks for nothin'!" she muttered.

Passing the large rock on the ledge proved easier for Brogan and his horse than it did for Annie. Brogan tried coaxing her round the edge, but she obstinately refused, insisting on climbing over. The problem was that once on top of the rock, she simply froze in horror, her eyes transfixed on the valley floor some two hundred feet below.

"Don't look down!" Brogan ordered. "Give me your hand!" Annie simply stayed frozen, not moving a muscle.

After alternately coaxing and cursing her, Brogan finally clambered up beside her and, quite brutally and suddenly, pushed her off on to the ledge. Her scream echoed around the valley as she thought she was going over the edge, but the only result of her experience was a couple of bruises and hurt pride.

Brogan jumped down beside her and shook his head as he helped her up. "One thing about it, if Carter or anyone else is within five miles, they sure know where we is now!"

"Sorry about that!" she choked. "I told you, I don't like heights, I just well . . . I just couldn't move!"

"It happens!" said Brogan, slipping his arm round her shoulders to comfort her. "Why the hell it has to keep happenin' to me though I just don't know. Sorry about pushin' you off like that but I thought it was the best way."

"It was a bit brutal, but it worked," she smiled weakly. "OK, I'm all right now, let's just get off this damned ledge!"

They continued along the narrow ledge with Brogan leading his horse and Annie following behind and holding tightly on to the horse's tail, which the horse thought was a distinctly bad idea and constantly tried to flick it out of her grasp. In actual fact she was in

greater danger of being whisked off
the ledge by the force of the horse's
tail than anything else. Brogan soon
realized this fact and ordered her not
to hold on. Very reluctantly she let go,
but still kept very close to the rear of
the horse.

Gradually the ledge widened out
until they had reached the point where
Brogan had originally made his way
up through the crevasse. He found
the way down into the crevasse easily
enough but, if anything, it was even
steeper and more slippery than the first
crevasse they had come down. Once
again Brogan had to keep his weight
against his horse and his feet braced
against the rock as they descended.
It took a long time, but they were
eventually on the more level, and
narrower, part of the crevasse. It was
a tight squeeze for the horse, but she
eventually managed to get through.

"Don't ever expect me to do any
climbin' again!" Annie choked as they
reached the valley floor. "I know it

seems childish to you, but that was just about the most terrifyin' thing ever!"

"Even worse'n bein' raped?" asked Brogan.

"That just hurt!" she said. "Goin' along that ledge was somethin' totally different. I ain't never been so scared."

"Well," said Brogan. "Shouldn't be no more need for you to go up or down. It's level all the way to Kenton from here on."

Brogan pulled Annie up behind him and briefly wondered if the two horses owned by the bounty hunters were still where they had been left. That was further up the valley and he had not seen any sign of them as they had passed up the spot while on the ledge so he decided that it was not worth the bother; it was not all that far to where he had left Annie's draught horse. They could collect that and take it into Kenton.

Brogan heard clearly enough: the only trouble was that he heard too late and Hank Carter was ordering

229

them to stop before Brogan could go for his gun. In any event his movements were hampered by having Annie behind him.

"Told you I'd get you!" said Carter, gleefully.

Brogan could tell quite easily where Carter was although he could not see him. It was one thing knowing where Hank Carter was, it was another knowing where his companion, the Irishman, was.

"You ain't got me yet!" replied Brogan.

"All I've got to do is squeeze this trigger!" gloated Carter.

"Then squeeze it!" invited Brogan. Annie clung even tighter to his waist.

Brogan had had years of learning about people and he considered himself a pretty good judge of character and the way a man's mind worked. Already he felt that he had a slight advantage. Had Carter simply been intent on killing him, the deed would have been done by now. Carter wanted to gloat and, more importantly as far as Brogan was concerned, ask questions. A talkative, inquisitive man could, and often did, lose his concentration and make mistakes.

"All in good time, my friend!" laughed Carter, appearing from behind a fallen tree. The Irishman was close behind, also holding a rifle. "First though, I'm curious. Just how the hell did you know where I was an' how the hell did you get there without bein' seen by either me or them others?"

"Them others were bounty hunters," said Brogan.

"I know that!" snapped Carter. "Don't tell me things I know already!" It was slight, but Brogan detected annoyance and decided that one way to rattle Carter was to tell him things he already knew. The only trouble with that approach was that he might just squeeze that trigger in annoyance.

"How'd you know?" asked Brogan, genuinely curious.

"Irish here, he knows them!" said

Carter, still holding a steady rifle on Brogan. "Surprisin' man is our Irish," continued Carter. "He knew who they were and he knew about that valley up there. I must admit I would never have found it in a million years."

"Wondered how you found it," said Brogan. "I found the place by followin' you, just like the bounty hunters did. Only one thing, why did it take you so long to get up there after you ambushed me? I'd been to Kenton an' back."

"Those bounty hunters were good!" admitted Carter. "I had to lead them on a pretty dance. I couldn't risk goin' straight up, they'd've followed me easy enough. They did follow, at least two of them did, but I killed them."

"I know, I saw," said Brogan.

"You saw?"

"Sure, I was just above them hidin' on a small ledge. I had to go up, I was between you an' them an' I didn't think either of you would ask me to move before shootin'."

"I guess that explains a lot!" grunted Carter. "I had this feelin' there was somebody there. Anyhow, McNally, your time has come: I'm goin' to kill you. Pity really, I kind of like you, but I can't forgive you for what happened in Appleby."

There were two shots, neither of them from either Hank Carter or the Irishman. Hank Carter's gun clattered to the ground and he swerved round clutching his shoulder. The Irishman, in contrast, slowly buckled at the knees, gently releasing his rifle. Both rifle and man met the ground at the same time. The only obvious injury to the Irishman was indicated by a trickle of blood oozing from the centre of his forehead.

Almost in the same instance as the shots, Brogan was leaping off his horse and racing towards Hank Carter, who offered no resistance as Brogan forced him to the ground, pulling Carter's Adams from its holster and holding it to Carter's head. For a very brief instant

Hank Carter glared pure hatred into Brogan's hard, steely eyes, but then he relaxed and even laughed derisively.

"Christ! I said it before an' I'll say it again!" Carter groaned. "You must have a guardian angel up there."

"Don't know about that," Brogan grunted. "Devil more like, so I've been told. This time though the angel was a human one!" He looked up at Annie who was still astride the horse holding Brogan's Colt which she had slipped from his holster. "Thanks . . . Annie . . . I guess that makes us even."

"Guess so," she agreed. "Can I put this gun down now?"

"Sure thing!" Brogan laughed, standing up himself and indicating that Carter did the same. "I know you said you knew how to handle a gun," Brogan continued. "Wasn't too sure if that was all talk or not. I apologize for any doubts I had. That was some fancy shootin', somethin' you don't often see in a woman, 'specially a city-bred woman."

"It was lousy shootin'," she said, laughing slightly. "He should've been dead, just like the other one."

"Yeh?" said Brogan. "Well . . . it was still pretty good shootin' anyhow."

Hank Carter was trying to stop the flow of blood from the wound in his shoulder and Brogan handed him a piece of rag from his pocket. "I must've had a black cat walk in front of me the day I met you!" Carter grated. "Have you been sent to plague me?"

"Seems to me it's you what's done all the plaguin'," said Brogan. "I just happened to be there."

"That's what I mean!" Carter muttered. "OK, so you take me in and from what I hear I'm worth, you'll be quite a rich man."

"Wouldn't know what to do with that much money," said Brogan. "'Sides, by rights it ain't me what's due for the reward, it's Annie here. I reckon she deserves it too, don't you? You shot her husband an' he may still die, I don't know. You raped her, kidnapped her . . . That's another thing. What you wanna do that for? She warn' no threat to you an' I don't reckon she's worth much as ransom."

Carter laughed, painfully. "I had some crazy idea of gettin' you through her."

"Yeh," Brogan grinned. "It's been tried before. Ain't worked yet, don't suppose it ever will. OK, where's your horses?"

Carter indicated behind him. "About two hundred yards!"

Brogan turned to Annie, almost apologetically. "I got to ask you to keep him covered while I go for the horses . . . " She nodded and raised the gun at Carter. "Just remember," Brogan said to Carter, "she ain't half a bad shot an' ain't afraid to shoot. She musta had lessons like you did." Carter simply scowled and continued trying to stem the flow of blood from his shoulder.

It took Brogan about ten minutes to return with the horses and he strapped the body of the Irishman across one and then indicated that Hank Carter should mount the other, which he did with a bit of help from Brogan.

"I thought you might leave this one behind, like you did the other," said Annie.

Brogan laughed. "This one's worth money, not a lot, but there ain't no sense in leavin' money lyin' around. I don't reckon the other one was worth anythin'."

"What about the buzzards?" Annie laughed, dryly.

"They'll survive!" Brogan grinned. "OK, let's move, we've still got a long ride to Kenton." He mounted the horse with the body strapped across its back, took his Colt off Annie and ordered Hank Carter to ride in front, with the threat of a bullet in his back if he tried to escape.

Brogan's senses were screaming at him and he ordered Carter to stop. He silenced a question from Annie and ignored a sneering comment from Hank Carter. There was danger up ahead, he knew it. Quite what had alerted him he had no idea, but there was definitely something. He pulled alongside Annie and addressed his own horse.

"You hear it too?" he asked the horse, much to the amusement of Annie and the mystification of Hank Carter. The horse responded by nodding firmly with its head and giving a slight snort.

"You don't really think she knows what you're talking about?" said Annie.

"You said that once before," said Brogan. "There's somethin' or someone up there. I sense it an' she does too, that's good enough for me."

"Somethin' or someone?" asked Annie.

"Most likely someone," said Brogan, "an' my guess is it's that other bounty hunter. He wants our friend Carter here. Only trouble is, I don't think he's the sort of feller who would worry too much if he just happened to kill us in the process."

"I hope he does!" scowled Carter.

"Yeh," agreed Brogan, "I 'spect you do, since you is more'n likely a dead man anyhow. If neither of us kills you, this bounty hunter might an' if he don't the law is almost certain to." He laughed lightly. "It must be kinda comfortin' knowin' exactly what your future is!"

Carter simply scowled and made no comment. "What are you goin' to do now then? Just sit here and wait? I'd rather take my chance and just run through."

"You could end up with a bullet in your back!" reminded Brogan. To accentuate the point he drew his Colt and indicated to Annie to take the Irishman's gun from his belt. "If we don't kill you, this Greasy Speak is more'n likely to."

"And I could just make it!" sneered Carter. Suddenly he spurred his horse into a gallop and raced on.

Brogan knocked Annie's gun down. "No, don't!" he ordered. "Come on, let's go!"

Even Brogan's old horse managed a fair gallop as they raced after Hank Carter, but still Brogan made no attempt to shoot. Suddenly there was a shot and Hank Carter twisted in the saddle, but he held on and continued his bid for freedom. Brogan waved Annie to follow while he veered off amongst some trees.

Greasy Speak had not been expecting either of these events, in fact he did not see Brogan until it was too late and Brogan was leaping off his horse to crash into him. There followed a brief tussle on the ground, but Brogan had winded Greasy when he had landed on him and was quickly standing over him, his Colt trained unerringly at his head. The bounty hunter realized that he was beaten and relaxed. Brogan picked up Greasy's rifle and Colt and threw them to one side.

"You!" grunted Greasy. "What the hell are you doin' here? I thought you'd gone to Kenton."

"I did," replied Brogan. "I had some

unfinished business though. Sorry about Hank Carter, you'll just have to admit this one got through your fingers."

"Could be he's got through yours too!" said Greasy.

"Doubt it!" said Brogan, confidently. "I reckon Annie's just about caught up with him by now. He's got two holes in him now, one Annie put there an' I reckon you just put another one in him."

"I hit him all right!" muttered Greasy. "I want that feller more'n I've ever wanted any outlaw." He struggled to his feet and eyed the gun in Brogan's hand warily. "He killed my partners!"

"I know," said Brogan. "I saw him kill the two on the ledge an' I found the body of the other one up the valley."

"I ain't bothered about the reward!" said Greasy. "Not this time. All I want to do is kill him!"

"Sorry, no can do," said Brogan. "We're takin' him in alive an' Annie's goin' to collect the reward. Now, just to make sure you don't cause no more trouble until we're in Kenton, I'm gonna tie you up . . . " Greasy looked at Brogan in alarm. "Don't worry, I'll tell that sheriff where you is."

"Ain't him I'm worried about," said Greasy. "It's wolves, there's a pack of 'em just moved in. Tie me up an' I'd be easy meat for 'em."

"Yeh," said Brogan. "I seen their tracks." He looked thoughtful. "OK, tell you what I'll do. I'll take your horse an' you can walk. I'll leave it at that farm between here an' Kenton; I hear the old man's some sort of kin of yours."

"Yeh, my mother's cousin or somethin'. Leave the horse, I won't stop you takin' Carter in."

"No deal," said Brogan, well aware that that was one promise which would be quickly broken. He walked to where he had thrown Greasy's guns and picked them up. "I'll leave these along the trail, 'bout a hundred yards or so, then you walk. That should give us time to get to Kenton."

"Bastard!" muttered Greasy. "I hope Carter's got away!"

Brogan shrugged and mounted his horse and went to collect Greasy's. He left the guns, as promised, about a hundred yards up the trail.

In the meantime, Annie had caught up with Hank Carter, who was slumped in his saddle. There did not seem to be much need to keep her gun trained on him; although he was still alive, he was certainly in a bad condition, oblivious to what was going on around him. She took hold of the reins and waited for Brogan, unsure if he would be coming or not.

"You had me worried!" she grinned as Brogan rode into view leading the bounty hunter's horse. "He's in a bad way." She nodded at the body slumped on the horse. "He might not make it alive."

"If he gets there dead, he's only worth a thousand," said Brogan. "But I reckon even a thousand will be of some use to you."

She shuddered slightly. "Blood money! I ain't too sure I want any part of it."

Brogan laughed. "I'll guarantee your principles will fly out the door when you see that money. I don't like bounty huntin' either, but I ain't averse to collectin' the odd reward when it comes my way. Wouldn't hunt a man just for the money though."

"I expect you're right!" she sighed. "OK, let's get to Kenton. You don't think anything else is goin' to happen do you?"

"Shouldn't think so!" Brogan was quite confident this time.

"He could've escaped," said Annie. "That was some chance you took. Why didn't you shoot when he started? You had the chance."

"It was a chance I was prepared to take," said Brogan. "I knew the bounty hunter was there an' I knew he wanted Carter." He smiled broadly. "Could have been awkward though, I was bankin' on Carter makin' a run for it. I ain't at all sure what I would've done if'n he'd stayed."

Annie shook her head. "There's two things that bug me about you. The first is talkin' to your horse as though she understands every word . . . "

"She does!" assured Brogan. "Got a whole lot more sense'n me sometimes too."

Annie laughed. "I can believe that too! The other thing that bugs me is just how the hell you seem to know there's someone up ahead. I can never hear a thing."

"Now that's somethin' I can't explain," admitted Brogan. "'Ceptin' I've spent most my life driftin' so I guess I just sorta picked it up. I even listen to the ground sometimes, old Indian trick. Most folk laugh at it, but it works." Annie was close by him and was sniffing the air. "Another thing," said Brogan. "I've got this ability to see into the future."

"Oh yeh!" she laughed.

"Yeh!" said Brogan, laughing with her. "Any time now you is gonna suggest I'd smell a whole lot sweeter if'n I was to take a bath with hot water an' real soap!"

She laughed again. "Yeh, you can read the future!"

THE END

**Other titles in the
Linford Western Library:**

TOP HAND
Wade Everett

The Broken T was big. But no ranch is big enough to let a man hide from himself.

GUN WOLVES OF LOBO BASIN
Lee Floren

The Feud was a blood debt. When Smoke Talbot found the outlaws who gunned down his folks he aimed to nail their hide to the barn door.

SHOTGUN SHARKEY
Marshall Grover

The westbound coach carrying the indomitable Larry and Stretch headed for a shooting showdown.

FIGHTING RAMROD
Charles N. Heckelmann

Most men would have cut their losses, but Frazer counted the bullets in his guns and said he'd soak the range in blood before he'd give up another inch of what was his.

LONE GUN
Eric Allen

Smoke Blackbird had been away too long. The Lequires had seized the Blackbird farm, forcing the Indians and settlers off, and no one seemed willing to fight! He had to fight alone.

THE THIRD RIDER
Barry Cord

Mel Rawlins wasn't going to let anything stand in his way. His father was murdered, his two brothers gone. Now Mel rode for vengeance.

ARIZONA DRIFTERS
W. C. Tuttle

When drifting Dutton and Lonnie Steelman decide to become partners they find that they have a common enemy in the formidable Thurston brothers.

TOMBSTONE
Matt Braun

Wells Fargo paid Luke Starbuck to outgun the silver-thieving stagecoach gang at Tombstone. Before long Luke can see the only thing bearing fruit in this eldorado will be the gallows tree.

HIGH BORDER RIDERS
Lee Floren

Buckshot McKee and Tortilla Joe cut the trail of a border tough who was running Mexican beef into Texas. They stopped the smuggler in his tracks.

BRETT RANDALL, GAMBLER
E. B. Mann

Larry Day had the choice of running away from the law or of assuming a dead man's place. No matter what he decided he was bound to end up dead.

THE GUNSHARP
William R. Cox

The Eggerleys weren't very smart. They trained their sights on Will Carney and Arizona's biggest blood bath began.

THE DEPUTY OF SAN RIANO
Lawrence A. Keating and
Al. P. Nelson

When a man fell dead from his horse, Ed Grant was spotted riding away from the scene. The deputy sheriff rode out after him and came up against everything from gunfire to dynamite.